Be sure to define the rules before you play…

Tristan will come out to his colleagues when he meets the right guy. He just hasn't met him yet.

Fidi, out and proud, plays a game with his colleagues to prove that they treat him differently because of his sexuality.

But what happens when someone doesn't play by the rules?

Flirting in PLAIN SIGHT

A French Office Romance

R.W. WALLACE

Flirting in Plain Sight
by R.W. Wallace

Copyright © 2019 by R.W. Wallace

Copy editing by Jinxie Gervasio
Cover Illustration 19292952 © wisiel | 123rf.com
Cover Illustration 109932412 © greens87 | 123rf.com
Cover by the author

All characters and events in this book, other than those clearly in the public domain, are fictitious and any resemblance to real persons, living or dead, is purely coincidental.

This book was first published in 2019 under the author name Eva Saint-Julien.

All rights reserved. No part of this publication may be reproduced, distributed, or transmitted in any form or by any means, including photocopying, recording, or other electronic or mechanical methods, without the prior written permission of the publisher, except in the case of brief quotations embodied in critical reviews and certain other noncommercial uses permitted by copyright law.

www.rwwallace.com

ISBN: [979-10-95707-65-3]

Main category—Fiction
Other category—Romance

First Edition

Don't miss the second book in the French Office Romance Series:

Like so many introverts, Laure has a secret persona online — one who writes romance. Every Saturday night, she gets comfortable with her blanket, her tea, and her laptop, and reads and writes love stories to her heart's content.

In real life, she has a crush on her colleague Denis. She'd love to be as forward and adventurous as her characters and flirt with the guy, but her shyness stops her from doing more than asking for his help on correcting today's bug.

Everything is going along just fine — until her two worlds start to overlap.

ONE

The First Thing You Think Of

"We've had a major security breach."

Dimitri Blanchequeue, director of my department and generally so busy that everybody knew who he was, but nobody had ever talked to him for more than two minutes, stared at me through his wire-rimmed glasses. His blue eyes were sharp and focused, and his bushy gray-streaked brows were drawn into a severe line across his forehead. He was handsome enough for a man in his mid-fifties, but the lines marking his face came from frowning, not smiling.

Our clothing reflected our difference in position; he wore his usual pinstriped suit, white shirt, and a boring but classy red tie. I wore dark blue jeans with a basic black leather belt and a fitted dark purple button-down shirt with the sleeves pulled up. We wore the same pointy black leather shoes, though. They went just as well with a suit as with a pair of jeans, and there was no way I'd ever show up to work in a pair of sneakers, no matter how fancy or expensive.

We occupied the building's second-largest meeting room. It was mostly used for trainings; the large table could comfortably receive twenty trainees with their laptops, and a coffeemaker stood ready in the far corner. The view wasn't much to write home about since we were in the basement and could only see the legs of the people walking past outside, but there were windows and they were facing south, so there was plenty of light.

Today, it was just the two of us, and Dimitri indicated I should sit down at the far end of the table, as far from the door as possible. I'd expected him to sit across from me so we'd be facing each other, but no, he'd pulled a chair right up next to mine, way into my personal space, and sat so close our knees almost touched.

I fiddled with my pen, clicking it open and closed. I hardly ever took any notes worth re-reading later, but having my hands occupied helped me sort through my thoughts and stay focused on the subject at hand.

Dimitri snapped the pen out of my hand, put it on my notebook, and pushed both out of my reach. "There will be no notes from today's meeting," he said.

"Okay, no problem." I folded my hands on the table in front of me, sending out choir boy vibes.

"We've had a security breach," Dimitri repeated, "and we need you to put out the fires before the client discovers the smoke."

I couldn't help but feel pride that they thought I was the right guy to fix whatever the problem was. I'd had nothing but positive feedback on my work during the six years I'd spent in this company, but it was the first time I'd been singled out for a specific task.

"What kind of security breach are we talking about?"

"Misplaced database with sensitive client data."

I raised by eyebrows. "Misplaced?"

Dimitri's gaze stayed on mine. I could have sworn he hadn't blinked since we sat down. "Somebody's trying to sell it to the highest bidder online."

I winced. "Ouch."

"Yes. Ouch. Now, I know it's probably redundant, but I'm going to say it anyway. What I tell you here today does not leave this room. There will be no notes and no talking about it over a cup of coffee with friends. No midnight discussion in bed about what happened at work today."

Well, that last one certainly shouldn't be a problem, unless they were worried my stuffed teddy bear would tattle to the client.

"And no telling the client about the breach until we've managed the situation."

I ran a hand over my scruffy jaw. Keeping my hands immobile just wasn't a possibility for me. "Which client are we talking about? This isn't on my current project?"

A curt shake of his head. "Of course not. We'll need you to leave your project effective immediately. Cécile can take over for you as Project Manager, right?"

The pleasure of being singled out dimmed somewhat. I'd worked my ass off for the past two years to get my team organized and effective—I didn't relish just ditching them at the drop of the hat because some other project had messed up. But Cécile, my second in command, was more than capable of taking over. In fact, I'd been worried she'd be moved to a different project for a couple of months because she wanted to be PM of her own project. Guess now she had it.

"Cécile will be perfect for the job," I said. I felt confident I'd kept any negative feelings from showing on my face.

Dimitri nodded. "The client is Thum Motors."

Shit. One of our biggest clients. A huge part of the French automotive market. Almost half our projects were for them, generating work for close to four hundred people. And if I remembered correctly… "We're up for renewal on several contracts with them this year, right?"

"Seven out of nine bundles."

My eyes went to the sliver of blue sky visible through the windows, but I wasn't really seeing it. "And if they react like Montagne Bleue…"

Dimitri nodded, and his eyes shone with approval. "Exactly."

Montagne Bleue was a telephone operator we'd worked for for years. A little over a year earlier, part of their database had been hacked and personal data of their clients had found its way into the wrong hands. Luckily, the security breach hadn't happened on any of our software, but we'd still had some backlash. Montagne Bleue had decided to audit all their subcontractors on security issues and we—along with most of the other subcontractors—had come up short. As a result, not only had we put in place a ton of actions to be up to par on security, but we'd been banned from answering any Requests For Proposals for six months.

If that happened with Thum Motors, the entire company would be in big trouble.

"Are we sure the leaked database is our fault?" I asked.

"Yes. We're the only ones working on this particular database. And to add insult to injury, it's clearly a database that's been tampered with for testing purposes, with names and information on our collaborators used to test certain functionalities. It'd be hard to explain that away."

"Shit." I ran both hands through my hair, probably making it even more messy than usual. I met Dimitri's blue eyes. "What do you want me to do?"

Dimitri rapped his knuckles on the table and shifted on his chair. He was getting ready to leave. "You're going to be the new PM of the project. What I need you to do is to put into place all the security measures we had to use with Montagne Bleue and make it seem like they've been in place for a while. The team needs to be trained on security issues, and they have to actually understand everything, not just sign a piece of paper saying they listened to you talk about the subject for an hour. We need to know who was responsible for the security breach and if they did it on purpose or if it was just stupidity. And we need to keep the information of the breach from the client for as long as possible—but with a plan in place for how to handle it when they do learn that their data is leaked."

I felt my mouth hanging open, but I couldn't even bring myself to shut it. "Is that all?" I whispered.

"Don't worry," Dimitri said. "You won't be working alone. I'm also bringing in a new Tech Lead. He's transferring in from our offices in Albi, so the chances of him being behind the leak are nil, and he's got lots of experience with applications security. He'll be a real asset to you."

I nodded as I ran a hand through my hair again.

"Maybe you know him?" Dimitri said. "His name is Fidisoa."

I shook my head. "Never heard of him." And with a name like that I would have remembered.

"No? He's gay."

And there it was. The reason I'd chosen not to be out in the workplace. How do you describe the guy? No hair or skin color, no size or personality trait. Just gay. It's the first thing people come up with to describe him.

Something must have shown on my face, because Dimitri hurried to add, "I'm not saying that to judge him in any way. It's just that he's…obvious about it, so it kind of sticks to your mind. He worked on a project here in Toulouse for a month last summer, so you could have crossed paths."

"I didn't think you were judging him," I said, though of course I did. "But I really don't think I know him." Because, yes, I would have noticed an "obviously" gay guy in our midst.

Dimitri studied me for a few seconds, but I had my poker face on now, not giving anything away. "Okay, perfect," he said finally. "We'll go meet the team straight away, and Fidisoa should be here this afternoon. He'll be the only other person knowing about our problem, so you two will probably spend quite some time together."

Somehow, that didn't really sound like a hardship. Which should have worried me but didn't.

As we walked toward the door, Dimitri slapped a hand on my shoulder. "Also, we need to tell the current PM that he's being replaced. He's not as organized as we'd hoped, so this has been in the cards for a while, but he probably won't be ecstatic about the news."

Great. As if this mission wasn't challenging enough.

TWO

Suddenly, the Name Made Sense

Olivier, the Project Manager I was to replace, was not happy about his change of status.

Dark eyes blazing, he stood just inside the door of Dimitri's office, hands on hips, making his rugby-playing shoulders look even wider than normal. "How can I get no say in this?" he gritted out through clenched teeth.

Had we been on a rugby field, I would have been running the other direction, but since I was fairly confident he wouldn't try to hit me in front of the big boss, I stood my ground. By which I mean I kept my mouth shut and let Dimitri do the talking while I leaned against the wall as if I got to listen in on someone being stripped of their PM status every day.

"You're free to tell me your opinion, Olivier," Dimitri said, calm and unruffled by the man towering above the both of us. "But this is neither the time nor the place. I think I've made it abundantly clear that it is in no way Tristan's fault that he's taking over as PM, so I know you will not take your frustration out on him."

Olivier opened his mouth to argue anyway, but Dimitri plowed right over him, proving that a suit could win over muscles if handled correctly. "Since the whole debacle with Montagne Bleue last summer, we've been on your case to implement all the necessary measures to clean up this project's act on security measures. As far as I can see, it still hasn't been done, even though we told the client that it was. I need someone in charge who will get things moving, and fast."

I fought not to shake my head at the mountain of muscles as I took in this new information. They'd told the client all security measures were in place only to discover that they were leaking like a sieve? I couldn't help but wonder if Olivier could possibly be the person behind the leak. And there was the reason for Dimitri's wish to keep Olivier on board, even though it meant a demotion for him.

God, this was going to be fun, getting to know the new team, and all the time wondering if *this* was the person who'd sold us out.

Olivier shifted from foot to foot and crossed his arms over his impressive chest, only to uncross them immediately. It looked like he realized this wasn't the best time to come off as too aggressive.

"We have started all the actions you told us to do," Olivier said to Dimitri. "The Security Assurance Plan is—"

"The Security Assurance Plan is still a draft," Dimitri said. "I looked at it, and it's just the company template with the name of the project on the first page. It doesn't have links to all the client's security requirements, and several sections that should be removed because they're not applicable to your project, are still there. Somebody spent all of five minutes on that task, then stopped. Three months ago."

Olivier eyed the door as if considering his chances if he made a run for it. "We installed the software for the static code checks—"

"The reports are generated every night, but nobody ever so much as opens them," Dimitri countered. "You don't even have anyone on your team who's trained to analyze them since you haven't sent any of them to the numerous training sessions available."

Ah man, I wouldn't even have anyone who knew what they should have been doing? This just kept getting worse.

Olivier's mouth moved, but nothing came out. I pitied the guy. But not too much, because I was the one who was going to clean up his mess.

"Olivier," Dimitri said, his voice uncharacteristically gentle. "We're not doing this to criticize you or to point any fingers. We're doing it because it's absolutely critical that we clean up all these security issues and come off as perfectly clean with the client. Our contract is up for renewal this year and we cannot allow for any slip-ups. So, you're going to work with Tristan here, and Fidisoa when he arrives, to help them understand everything about the project and the people. I can count on you for this, yes?"

Olivier's shoulders slumped, if that could really be said of such a mass of muscle, and he nodded curtly.

I let out a relieved breath. "Thank you. I'm sure we'll get along just—"

The office door slammed open, followed by a tenor voice yelling, "Shit, I'm sorry! I didn't expect the door to actually open."

And in came the gay guy.

About my height, slim but not skinny, dark luminous skin I hoped he spent hours tending to or life just wasn't fair, large eyes so dark they might as well be black, and perfectly coiffed hair with just a hint of a curl on top. And highlights. He wore the classic engineer uniform of jeans, leather shoes, and button-down shirt, but there was something more…studied…about the way he wore it than Olivier and me.

He was your stereotypical gay, and he was gorgeous. Malagasy, if I wasn't mistaken. Suddenly, the name made sense.

"Fidisoa," Dimitri said, completely unruffled by the abrupt interruption. "I'm so glad you could make it on such short notice. Please come in, and close the door behind you?"

"Sure." Fidisoa flashed a knee-weakening smile before gently closing the door. "Please, call me Fidi."

Dimitri waved a hand at Olivier. "Fidisoa, please meet Olivier Charles, former PM on the project you'll be working on. And Tristan Marty, the new PM."

Smile still in place, Fidi shook Olivier's hand, only a slight wince indicating that the brute must have attempted to crush the smaller man's hand. Then he stepped across the room, moving with the grace of a dancer, to greet me.

Heart beating hard in my chest like it always did when I was too near a gorgeous guy, I managed to keep my voice steady as my hand fit perfectly into his. "*Enchanté.*"

"So," Fidi said as he shook hands with Dimitri. "What do I need to know?"

Dimitri knocked his knuckles on his desk. "Tristan will fill you in. Now." He stood, making all three of us instinctively move toward the door. "I've made reservations for the entire team at the restaurant just across the street, *la Table Gourmande*. The company will pay for the today's specials for everyone, and one drink." He looked to Fidi and I. "Take the opportunity to get to know the team."

"Excellent," Fidi exclaimed, smile still flashing. "I didn't get the time to have breakfast this morning. I'm starving." He was the first out the door, and Olivier followed with a scowl and his hands jammed into his jeans' pockets.

I followed suit, but Dimitri spoke before I was out the door. "Keep me posted on your progress, all right, Tristan? Only in person, not in writing. And close the door on your way out."

THREE

Why Would You Dress Like That if You Never Get Laid?

THE TEAM CONSISTED of six developers and two functional analysts. I found myself at the middle of the table, squeezed between Olivier and Fidi, with three developers across from us.

Laure, a pretty brunette with hipster glasses and a flower barrette, had been on the project for three months and it was her first job. She seemed capable and aware of the fact that she had lots to learn before becoming an expert. She didn't ask any questions about why I was suddenly going to take over Olivier's job when he obviously didn't have any new and fancy position to go to, which I appreciated but also found slightly alarming.

Next to her, Denis, in his late twenties with a pronounced bald patch he might want to cover up by shaving his head soon, had almost ten years of Java under his belt, which meant he'd learned to code before becoming a student. He seemed to be career-focused, but clearly aimed for the position of technical expert. He kept stealing glances at Fidi, and I had a feeling it wasn't because of the new Tech Lead's pretty face.

Finally, the last member of the team I was able to talk with during the meal, Mathieu. Probably closing in on thirty-five, with lots of technical experience, but he'd also been in charge of working with the Indians on his previous project, so he had managing experience. His unfriendly glances were only for me. Guess he'd been ready to step in whenever Olivier was dethroned. I'd have to make an extra effort in befriending him, to make sure he didn't try to sabotage my work.

Out of the three, I figured Denis was the least likely to be our culprit, because I just couldn't see what was in it for him—although he might be the best placed to know how to go about actually selling the data without it being traced back to him.

Laure was fresh and innocent and might not realize the gravity of what she was doing when she stole the database, and her arrival coincided with the date Dimitri had given me as an estimated time of the crime.

Mathieu…well, Mathieu could theoretically benefit from the kind of situation we were in right now, where Olivier had to step down because he hadn't managed his job well enough. But he hadn't factored in that the directors would want someone they were certain were innocent to take the lead.

"All right," Fidi spoke up beside me to be heard over the noise of the restaurant and the chatter of our new colleagues. "Who drinks what? This nice lady is ready to take our order."

Indeed, the waitress stood at the other end of the table, notebook in hand.

"The company is paying?" Denis asked.

"Yes," I said. "One drink each and the today's specials."

Laure grinned like it was Christmas and touched the large, blue flower of her barrette as if checking it was still in place above her ear. "Sweet. I'll have a kir, please."

The other girl, a woman in her mid-twenties named Sylvie, and Fidi ordered the same, and the guys each chose a beer. Could they all be more stereotypical? Should I order a beer to put myself in the camp of the straights? Or a kir to show my true colors? I shook my head at my own idiotic thoughts and ordered a Coke. Alcohol at lunch was not a good idea for me, especially since I was going to need all my mental capacities this afternoon.

Fidi took charge of taking everyone's orders for the food as well. With a smile and a wink at the waitress as she left, he leaned back in his seat and put a hand on his lean stomach. "Man, I'm starving. Dimitri called me at seven this morning, telling me to come here instead of the Albi offices, so I took off without having breakfast."

"I'm sure we could have waited another twenty minutes for you to have breakfast," I said, taking the opportunity to admire his smooth jaw.

Fidi widened his eyes at me. "Twenty minutes? What do you eat for it to take that long to wolf down?"

I had to smile at his reaction. It was half serious—he must down a couple of biscuits in the morning and call it breakfast—and half performing to make the rest of us laugh. He was clearly the type of guy who worked hard at putting everyone else at ease and did it perfectly.

"I need my twenty minutes to down a bowl of cereal and a large cup of coffee," I said. "We can't all jump out of bed looking like we stepped out of the cover of GQ."

"Hah! You wish," Fidi exclaimed with glee as he clapped his hands and jumped in his seat like an excited toddler. "I did take twenty minutes this morning, but it was in front of the mirror, and not in the kitchen."

See? I knew he worked to get skin that perfect.

Olivier spoke up for the first time since we'd left Dimitri's office. "Are you gay?" He sat huddled in on himself on the bench next to me, but even so, he took up more than his fair share of the space. He made muscles look like a burden, not a boon.

"Well, that's direct," I muttered. I avoided looking at Fidi in case he felt put on the spot by the question.

Fidi just barked out a laugh that had the group at a nearby table turning to see what was up. "Am I gay? Of course I'm gay." He laughed so hard his face was close to smashing into his plate and he held a fist to his stomach. "Ah, man, you're precious. No sane straight guy would look like this. He'd never ever get laid."

Olivier had a slight blush high on his cheeks, but he didn't back down. "Why would you dress like that if you never get laid?"

I'd had the misfortune of taking my first sip of Coke, and at Olivier's question, the drink promptly made its way up my nose. Bubbles and Coke through the nose? Not so much fun. Luckily, nobody seemed to notice my dilemma since they were all staring at either Olivier on my one side, or at Fidi on my other.

Fidi somehow managed to keep a straight face as he reached across me to lay a hand on Olivier's forearm. "My dear boy, you're a sweetheart. I said a *straight* guy wouldn't get laid looking like this. That's because as a *gay* guy, I most definitely do."

It was my turn to blush and I did my best to hide it behind my glass.

With a jerk, Olivier moved his arm away from Fidi's touch. There was no trace of disgust on his face, but he was clearly uncomfortable with the skin on skin contact.

"And that's one," Fidi said lightly. He glanced at his watch, the same Fitbit I used, but with a flashy, sparkling strap instead of the basic plastic black one I'd kept. "Less than thirty minutes. I think that might be record."

Laure had already downed half her drink and was running a finger around the rim as she looked from Fidi to Olivier. "A record for what?"

Olivier turned to his left, basically showing me his impossibly large back, to talk to the guy sitting on his other side. Getting out of the uncomfortable discussion with Fidi. Couldn't really blame him, honestly.

I crossed my arms and stared at Fidi. "Are you really making a sport of making people uncomfortable because you're gay?"

The beginnings of a smile formed on Fidi's lips, though he fought it by pursing them. He gave me a look that was downright flirty. "Maybe?" He rolled his eyes. "It's not like I go around feeling people up or anything. I'm just observing how long it takes with me behaving in a way that would be just fine from other people before they become all flighty."

"To be fair," Mathieu chimed in, "you did touch him."

Again with the eye roll. "My fingers grazed his arm. Are you telling me he would have jumped like that if it had been Laure, a pretty young girl, who'd touched him?"

Mathieu looked from Laure, who was once again touching her flower barrette, to Olivier, now talking to the other half of the table. "Yeah, no, probably not."

"Still," I insisted. "We're at work."

Fidi patted my hand, where it rested next to my glass, making the hairs on my arms stand to attention. "Don't worry, Tristan.

I can be professional. I won't make anyone uncomfortable or force myself on the straight dudes. I just take note when guys react differently to me than to other guys because of my sexuality. As if little me would be capable of forcing myself on someone of Olivier's caliber." He made a flexing movement to show how far he was from Olivier's size and I couldn't help a giggle from escaping.

Fidi squeezed my hand before retreating to his own space. "That's so cute. And congrats, by the way, on not flinching or moving your hand away or anything."

I gave him a mockingly stern stare. "Come now, Fidi. It's going to take more than a graze of hands to scare me."

His eyes gleamed as he wiggled his eyebrows. "Is that a challenge?"

"I don't bait that easily," I said, nonchalantly taking a sip of my Coke.

"Hmm. Really." His smile was sly and gorgeous and made my heart take a backward flip.

This new mission was looking brighter by the moment.

FOUR

I Love Having a Crush

I'D ALWAYS ENJOYED having a crush on someone.

In school, I'd invariably had my eyes on one guy or another, spending my days stealing glances at him and daydreaming about kissing, holding hands, you name it. I never expected it to actually lead to anything, and not only because I was, as far as I knew, the only gay guy in school. I just enjoyed the rush of those moments when my eyes met his across the room. I enjoyed memorizing the shape of his neck or the color of his eyes. It was innocent, and purely unrequited, and it helped me get through boring classes and never-ending lectures.

Once I'd started working, I'd kept up the habit. Basically, there was always some guy I was crushing on, though I was a lot more careful. I did *not* want to get caught.

Flirting in Plain Sight

In school, I'd been out since early high school. At work, I was in the closet. I always figured that if I ended up finding *the* guy, I'd tell people at work, but as long as I wasn't in a serious relationship, I didn't see why I should tell my colleagues about my sexual orientation. Once you were out, you were out. You couldn't show up the next day and say, actually, I was just kidding, I'm not actually gay. Also, and I knew this was me making excuses, but it was my life: I'd never told anyone I was straight, nor denied being gay—as if anyone would actually straight out ask that question of a colleague—I just kept my private life private, and people respected that.

Today, I'd found myself a new crush.

Fidi sat across from me in the huge meeting room in the basement. I'd taken a leaf out of Dimitri's book and chosen this room to make sure we wouldn't be overheard. I had just explained everything I knew about the security breach to Fidi and he sat with his elbows on the table and his fingers lodged in his hair.

I wanted to lodge my fingers in there myself. It looked really soft.

"*Putain*," he said as he shook his head gently. "We've certainly got our work cut out for us, don't we?"

I smiled at him. "We certainly do. You don't have a family to go home to, do you? I suspect we'll be pulling long hours." I'd meant it as a joke, but I found myself holding my breath waiting for his answer.

Fidi pulled his hands out of his hair and winked at me. "Fishing to know if I'm single?"

Thank God he'd pulled that stunt with Mathieu in the restaurant earlier, or I'd have thought I'd bleeped on his gaydar. I was fairly certain he was just pushing to see what it took to get me freaked out about him being gay. Good luck with that.

I leaned toward him over the table and flashed by biggest and fakest smile. "Well, are you?"

And damn it, I really did want to know.

He blinked twice, then his gorgeous smile came back online. "Free as a bird. I don't even have a cat to feed, so nobody will miss me if I don't come home every night."

I let my lust show for just a second but added a wink to make it seem fake. "Good to know."

Fidi burst out laughing, throwing his hands in the air and almost making his chair trip over backward. "Okay," he said once he was back in control. "You know how to play. I think we'll get along just fine."

I smiled back at him, happiness coursing through me. Crushing on a gay guy just might be a ton more fun than my usual straight targets.

"All right, back to business," I said. "Here's how I propose we do this."

Normally, I'd write all this down because I like having a trace of everything that's decided, but we were not to keep any trace of the fact that we knew there'd been a breach, so I just doodled in my notebook to keep my hands busy.

"As Tech Lead, you'll need to know the application and the code anyway, so I think you should start with that. While you're at it, you should try to evaluate who has the knowledge to pull off this stunt. Also, get to know the guys. We need to think about who would be stupid, brave, or greedy enough to do this, and I suspect they'll talk more to you than to me."

Fidi stared at me for a beat. "Why?"

I could feel in his gaze and his tone that he suspected I thought people would be more open to talk to a gay guy. He just might be a tad too hung up on the issue.

"Because I'm the boss," I said with a sigh. "I'm usually pretty hands-on and close to my guys, but I have to work for it and I'm not sure I'll have the time for that right now."

He nodded. "Fair enough. By the way, you are aware that there are two women on the team? I'm not sure you should be calling them 'guys.'"

I rolled my eyes at him. "I've been calling my team guys for years and there's always been at least one girl. Nobody's ever had a problem with it."

"Nobody's ever had a problem with my little game," Fidi countered.

Choosing to ignore his comment, I continued down my mental list. "I'll need to be in on all future meetings with the client and make sure they think that all the measures we're going to put into place now have actually been there for months. I'll need to be in his good graces for when this thing blows up in our faces."

"Yeah," Fidi agreed. "It's definitely going to blow up some day."

I nodded. "It's just a question of when." I started in on a new doodle on my notebook because the first one was looking more and more like Fidi's hair. "I'll write the Security Assurance Plan. I'll just need you to review it when I'm done."

"Sure."

"And you'll set up the tools to produce status reports on the security level of our code." I sighed as I met Fidi's eyes. "Depending on what you find, we might need to consider creating some false reports dating some time back. But I'm not exactly ecstatic about downright lying, so we'll cross that bridge when we come to it."

Fidi flipped back a page in his own notebook. "If I have the dates right, there hasn't been a delivery since the data were stolen. We're only supposed to produce the reports for delivery. So if we set things up quickly, we can correct the biggest security risks and pretend it's been in place since the first day after the last version. We're not beholden to them to give them all the details of what happens between deliveries."

"Fair enough." I tapped my pen on the table, trying to remember everything on my mental list from that morning. This mission was going to force me to work on my short-term memory. "Do you have anything to add?"

A flicker of satisfaction flashed in his eyes; he was happy I'd asked his opinion.

"We're only going to figure out who did it by getting to know the team better," he said. "What do you think our chances are of getting a Team Building weekend paid by the company?"

I nodded as I considered his words. "That's a great idea. An entire weekend living on top of each other and hanging out 24/7? I'd say it has a good chance of giving results. I'll air the idea with Dimitri."

"Great." Fidi straightened his shirt as he got ready to stand up. "Let's just hope nobody has any problems with sharing a room with the gay guy."

I hesitated as I straightened and gathered my notebook and phone. "You do realize you might be taking the whole gay thing a little far?"

Fidi squared his shoulders. No sign of his smile now. "I don't do the whole flamboyant thing for fun. It's who I am."

"Easy, Fidi," I said, my voice calm and a hand stretched toward him. "I'm not talking about that. You are who you want to be, and nobody here is judging you for it. I'm talking about the way you baited Mathieu at lunch. And that comment about sleeping in the same room as you was kind of…judgmental, considering you don't even really know the team yet."

I could see Fidi's jaw working as he considered my words. Finally, in an uneven voice, he said, "You don't know what it's like."

Actually, I did, but I wasn't about to tell him that. "I probably don't," I said instead. "I'm just asking you to give the team a chance. Maybe we won't reject you."

His eyes lit up and he seemed to be actually *seeing* me for the first time when I included myself in the group. "Or we'll see that's exactly what they'll do. I'll make sure you're around as a witness when I get too close to the guys." He chewed on his lip for a second, making me lose my train of thought. "Since you're so confident, if we get this Team Building weekend, you'd be up for sharing a room with me?"

"Of course." Since he was watching me very closely, I made sure not to show any emotion. Of course, he was looking for fear or disgust, while I was hiding excitement. My inner teenage girl was screaming her head off.

Fidi kept his gaze on me as he moved toward the door. "I'll hold you to that, *chef*."

"Deal," I said, following him out into the corridor. "But please don't start calling me boss. The others might pick up on it and I'll never be seen as one of the team."

"Sure thing, *chef*," he replied lightly.

As I followed him down the corridor toward the stairs, I had a new spring in my step and my heart was doing somersaults.

I loved having a crush.

FIVE

Three Down, Four to Go

Fidi didn't waste any time showing me how the guys on the team were uncomfortable with his gayness. At least, that's what it was in his head. I had to admit that if some random guy had come up to me and done the things he did, I probably would have stepped away, too. Being tolerant of other people being gay wasn't equivalent to wanting them in your personal space all day long.

Luckily, he went about it in a humorous way, making it a running joke for the team within less than twenty-four hours.

When Denis showed him the Wiki, explaining how they'd organized it and the stuff that still wasn't quite up to par, Fidi leaned over Denis' shoulder to shove his face close to the screen. He put a hand on Denis' shoulder as he read what was on the screen. Denis leaned away to avoid having his face shoved into Fidi's chest.

"Aw," Fidi said, giving Denis an overly theatric look. "Am I making you uncomfortable?"

Denis chuckled awkwardly.

Laure stepped in to save him. "Anyone would be awkward in that position," she said, laughter in her voice. She touched her barrette, today with a pink flower of some sort. "You do realize we're at work, right?"

Denis sent her a grateful look and the softest smile I'd seen on the guy since I'd met him. I suspected he had a crush on the girl, but a lot less confident the feeling was mutual.

Straightening, Fidi flashed them both one of his blinding smiles. "No worries. I'm not forcing myself on anyone. It's all in good fun, right?"

Denis snorted, but his smile stayed in place, and the handover of Wiki information went smoothly after that.

A couple of hours later, Fidi stood too close to Mathieu while waiting his turn at the coffee machine. He didn't actually touch the other man, but he was close enough for Mathieu to notice his presence, probably because of body heat. When he discovered Fidi standing there, he instinctively took a step back, knocking into the wall. Fidi had him walled in, which was funny considering Mathieu was half a head taller.

"Oh, I'm sorry," Fidi said. "Am I standing too close?"

At first, Mathieu seemed uncomfortable, but it didn't take long for him to crack a smile. "Yeah, just a tad. Didn't anyone teach you about personal space?"

Fidi grinned. "Nah." He stepped back to let Mathieu get his coffee.

As Mathieu passed me on his way out of the break room, he met my eyes and chuckled as he raised his eyebrows. "The new Tech Lead is kinda weird."

"I know," I replied. "But I'm thinking he'll grow on us."

Mathieu huffed a laugh. "Yeah. Seems likely."

I approached Fidi, who was sweet-talking the coffee machine to get it to work faster. "That's right, give me the magical poison." He glanced up at me. "Three down, four to go. No, five. Can't forget the new boss." He winked.

I cocked my head. "Really, you think this is an adult way to behave?"

He tipped his head from side to side as he considered. "Nah, not really. But it's fun. And don't worry, I'm good at detecting the guys who really do have a big problem with me, and I won't go anywhere near one of those. None of them on the team, I'm happy to report."

"Well, that's good to know," I said dryly.

The machine beeped to indicate the coffee was ready. "Yes yes yes," Fidi chanted and extricated the plastic cup as if it would blow up in his face if he wasn't careful. His moan of satisfaction once he took his first sip made my brain go offline for a moment.

"Were you getting a coffee?" Fidi asked me. He was looking at me oddly, making me realize I'd just stood there looking into space.

"Yeah." I inserted a euro into the slot and pushed the button for a cappuccino. "So, you're not going to stop your baiting?" I asked.

He considered me over the rim of his cup. "Does it really bother you that much?"

I shrugged. "Not really. Not yet? I don't know. I guess I'm just worried you'll go too far with someone and we'll have a harassment case on our hands. Or someone wanting to leave the team."

Fidi patted my forearm. "Don't you worry, Tristan. I know what I'm doing. I've done this since forever, and it's never gone too far. I'm good at reading people."

Sighing, I leaned down to get my cappuccino. "At least I tried."

Fidi downed the rest of his coffee and threw the plastic cup in the trash. "Duly noted. Also," he added over his shoulder as he left the room, "good job on not flinching."

I finished my coffee alone, going from reliving the thrill of my crush touching me, to worrying that he might have realized I was far from disgusted by him, to worrying his behavior would somehow undermine the work we had to do. The worry really should have won out.

But it didn't.

SIX

How Am I Supposed to React?

Saturday night found me sprawled on my friend Claire's couch, watching some action movie she'd chosen, but not following the plot in the slightest. I was exhausted from my first week with the new team, enough so that one beer had me slightly woozy.

"So, how's the new team?" Claire asked as some car chase in the movie went on and on. She had a beer in one hand and was wearing her usual Saturday night sweatpants and old t-shirt. She loved primping up, but after doing it every day of the week for work, she usually went in the extreme opposite direction on weekends when she had no other plans than to hang out with me and went with the most comfortable clothes she had. Her short black hair looked impeccable, as always, but it was more due to the haircut that basically managed itself, than to any work on her part. When she made an effort, I knew she used stuff in her hair, but it all looked the same to me. Not that I'd ever tell her that.

"They're all right," I replied. "Everybody seems fairly capable and mostly willing to actually work. They just need to be pushed in the right direction, and we'll be fine." I'd told her I'd been put on a new project to fix the last Project Manager's lack of leadership, but not that we had the threat of the security breach hanging over us.

"Good for you," Claire said and patted my knee. "Any cute guys?" Her brown eyes twinkled.

"Yes." I couldn't help but giggle.

Claire grinned and made a *go ahead* gesture with her free hand.

"Actually, there are several," I said. "This one guy, the deputy PM, Mathieu, is pretty cute. Tall, wiry, dark hair; all the stuff I usually like."

"But he's not the one you're crushing on." She knew me too well. We'd been friends since high school, and I'd told her of my tendency to always crush on someone about ten minutes after we met. Ever since, she'd demanded to get all the details, see the photos, meet the guys when possible. She'd met all my past boyfriends, too, of course, and if for some reason she didn't like the guy I introduced her to, it was as good as a death sentence to the relationship. I didn't dump the guys *because* Claire didn't like them, but if she raised the red flag, chances were I'd realize what she'd snagged on was a real problem, and within a week, I was single again.

"No," I said with a sigh. "And that would, in any case, have been awkward since I sort of bypassed him for the role of PM."

"Hey, angry sex can be fun."

"Yeah, no," I said. "Not my thing."

Claire nudged my leg with hers. "So, who's the lucky guy?"

I huffed. "You say that like my crush is actually going to have any sort of influence on his life. We're talking about work here, you know as well as I do that nothing's going to happen. Just some daydreaming on my side."

Claire's voice was much softer than usual. "I still say he's lucky to have your attention."

I shot her a smile, touched by her friendship. I cleared my throat. "Anyway, a new Tech Lead started on the same day as me," I said. "His name is Fidi, short for Fidisoa. He's Malagasy, so his last name is endless and I haven't even tried to pronounce it yet."

"Oh, Malagasy," Claire cooed. "I bet he's real pretty. Should be right up your ally."

I didn't even bother to fight down the grin that stretched across my face.

"Does he have a girlfriend?"

I knew she didn't really care if the guy was taken or not, she was just preparing for the day when I ended up spending an evening with my crush all over his significant other. She was the one to pick up the pieces, every single time.

"Single," I replied. "And…ah…that would be no boyfriend."

Claire's eyebrows shot up and she turned on the couch to face me fully, the movie completely forgotten. "He's gay?"

"Obviously so," I said. "And not making the slightest attempt to hide."

"Shit." Claire's eyes flicked back and forth as she thought. "Are there any other out guys in your company?"

I shook my head. "None that I know of."

"And how many employees are there, again?"

I knew where she was going with this. It was hardly the first time we discussed the subject. "About fifteen hundred in the Toulouse branch. Which means, of course, that statistically speaking, there should be more than one gay guy." I was certainly far from the only guy hiding his sexuality from his colleagues. But there was no way of figuring out who the others were without outing myself in the process.

"And this Fidi, he's not hiding at all?"

"No." I smile as I think of him and his antics. "I'm guessing he's one of those guys who doesn't really need to come out of the closet. When everybody's just, 'oh, was it supposed to be a surprise?' when he made the announcement."

"So, like at least three of your exes?" Claire's smirk should have been annoying, but it just made me grin right back.

"Yes, like that." What could I say? I wasn't one of the obvious ones myself, but they were who I tended to fall for. In a way, it was the reason for several of my break-ups, because the guys I was with couldn't understand why I didn't want to be out at work. I'd always tried to explain that I probably would come out one day, when I was sure the relationship would last. Which, of course, brought on the conversion of where we were going, and since I hadn't been confident in any of those relationship to go official, I'd been summarily dumped.

Claire folded her legs under her and took a sip of her beer. "So, what's he like?"

I groaned as I covered my eyes with my hand. "He's coming on to all the guys on the team to prove they're uncomfortable with being close to the gay guy."

Claire threw back her head and let out a peal of laughter. "Really? How do the guys react?"

"Not too bad, I guess. None of them have come to me complaining yet, at least."

"Has he done it to you?"

I ran a hand through my hair as my eyes widened at the thought. "No. I guess there's a possibility he'll avoid me since I'm the boss." I considered for a moment. "Actually, he's probably keeping me for last."

"And how do you think that'll go down?" Claire was completely ignoring the movie she'd insisted we watch, having apparently decided my life was better entertainment.

"Shit, I don't know." I met my friend's gaze, panic coursing through me. "How am I supposed to react?"

"Well, you could always take the opportunity to kiss him."

There was no way to qualify the sound that came out of my mouth. Mirth, panic, want. It all mixed to make my heart speed up and my stomach clench.

Claire tapped her bottom lip with a manicured finger. "You know, you could probably have some fun with this without necessarily outing yourself."

"What do you mean?"

"He gets physically close, to see when they step away, right?"

I nodded.

"Well, just never step away," she said. "See how close he's ready to come. I mean, if he wants to keep his job, he's not going to go as far as kissing or anything that could qualify as sexual harassment, so I don't think you need to worry about that." She grinned from ear to ear and made a *voila* gesture. "Call his bluff. And have some fun in the process."

Huh. That might actually work. It would allow me to keep the upper hand and perhaps show Fidi how silly that game of his was.

Also, I'd get to be close to Fidi without fear of discovery. Although I realized there were hundreds of ways this plan could backfire, I could already tell I'd do it. My smile stretched so wide it almost hurt.

Claire clapped her hands and let out a whoop. She pointed at me. "I'll expect updates. And see if you can get me a picture, will you?"

SEVEN

There Are Five Colors in the World

I'D BEEN RIGHT about Fidi keeping me for last. He'd gotten to the rest of the guys of the team by touching their arms, standing too close, or in one case, by bending over to pick up a pen he'd dropped on purpose, basically shoving his ass in the poor guy's face.

And then, it was my turn.

Dimitri had found my weekend Team Building to be an excellent idea and had sent me a list of three places that had openings on short notice. All expenses would be paid by the company. I called Fidi over to my desk to show him the three options we had for the Team Building weekend coming up. I shared the space with Denis, Mathieu, Fidi, and Laure, and the afternoon had been calm, all of us allowing the afternoon sun slanting through the suddenly very visibly dirty windows to lull us into a half-asleep state.

"What do you think?" I asked Fidi as he sauntered over and leaned down to look at my screen. "Spelunking, hiking, or off-road biking?"

At first, I didn't understand what was going on. One moment I had a perfect view of my screen and some dust motes dancing around in a ray of sunlight, and the next, all I could see was Fidi's green shirt. Then I caught a whiff of his cologne and some citrusy smell that was probably his shampoo and I felt like I'd stepped into a dream land. I half expected to hear a waterfall next.

Luckily, my face was hidden from the three other persons in the office, or I would have given myself away.

As it was, since Fidi planted his chest in my face and then just stayed put, I had the time to school my features into something that didn't scream happy and turned on.

"I don't think spelunking's a great idea," Fidi said casually. "Laure's afraid of water. What's this option?"

I assumed he was pointing at something on the screen. "I wouldn't know," I said, laughter in my voice. "Something's blocking my view."

"Huh," Fidi said. "That's weird."

"Yeah. And green."

Fidi straightened enough for him to meet my gaze. "This is pistachio, not green."

I deliberately let my eyes wander across his chest, and even lingered on his waist. "Green."

Rolling his eyes like a high schooler, Fidi went back to blocking my view. "To straight guys there are, like, five colors in the world."

This was getting ridiculous. We both had work to do, and I had a feeling he planned to stay where he was until I asked him to give me some space. Which, of course, I had no intention of doing.

I placed my hands on Fidi's hips. "If you need to be that close," I said as if all I wanted was to make him more comfortable, "why don't you come sit right here." And I pulled him into my lap.

The surprise on his face was priceless. His beautiful dark eyes went wide, and his lips parted on a gasp. His hands went straight out in front of him as if he didn't know where to put them and was afraid to touch anything by accident.

I adjusted him so he sat sideways on my lap, my left arm around his waist and my right hand on his knee. "That better?" I nodded at the screen. "You'll need to look that way if you want to keep reading, though."

Denis and Mathieu had both been focused on Denis's screen for the past half hour. Now they paused their conversation to stare at us in surprise.

Laure, alone at her desk in the far corner, giggled into her hand.

Fidi's mouth was working and after several attempts, he finally got a word out. "But…"

"Seriously, Fidi," I said, pointing at the screen. "That way. Hiking or biking?" I squeezed his thigh, delighted at the muscle I felt under the rough fabric of his jeans. He had the type of physique that could either come from good genes and no sports, or skinny genes and lots of sports. I was going to bet on the latter. Which gave my mind plenty of ideas—to contemplate later, when half my team wasn't looking.

Fidi finally snapped back to life. He didn't look at the computer, though, but kept his eyes on me, making my entire chest light up with pleasure. "I think we should go with hiking.

Everybody knows how to walk and nobody will have a sore ass after the first day."

I couldn't stop my eyebrows from shooting up at that.

Fidi burst out laughing, his hands coming up to frame his face. Laure followed suit with a high-pitched giggle, and the sounds coming from Denis and Mathieu's side of the room were somewhere between mirth and disgust. I didn't want to know.

Laughter fading, Fidi clapped his hands and jumped down from my lap. "All right, *chef*," he said. "You win the first round."

"The first round?" I extended my arms in appeal, doing my best to ignore how empty and cold my lap felt without him. "Why do you need several rounds?"

He just shook his head at me. "You've seen me do this to the rest of the team and were clearly prepared. I'm not buying that as your real reaction."

True. My real reaction would be to draw him even closer and to flirt my ass off. Ass-pinching wouldn't be off the table.

"Maybe you should see someone for this fixation of yours," I said, only half joking. "I can't believe it's never backfired on you."

A cute frown wrinkling his forehead, Fidi waved at my lap. "Well, it just did."

"I meant as in getting a fist in the face or a lawsuit against you." I kept my smile but tried to get him to understand I was perfectly serious.

He just shrugged. "Don't worry about it. I'm good at reading people."

I had my doubts about that, but I let the issue rest. One thing was for sure: his gaydar wasn't worth shit.

EIGHT

You're Not My Type

Ten days after my arrival in the new team, I was to meet the client. It was just a regular bimonthly meeting that Olivier had organized with the client since the beginning of time. Our challenge was to explain why I was there without giving away our security problems.

Dimitri must have worked on Olivier since that first day because he was now open to leaving the project in order to try his hand as Project Manager on a smaller team, one with less risks.

It was so much easier to explain to the client why the PM was leaving if we could truthfully say that he had a new project lined up. This was, after all, one of the only advantages with working for a subcontractor in Toulouse—the possibility to easily change projects. It was rare for anyone, even managers, to stay in one place for more than two or three years.

Figuring we might as well explain all the changes at once, we would also tell them that we had a new Tech Lead. Arguing this one was a little more complicated since we actually wanted Denis to stay on the team. So we were going to attempt selling them on having two Tech Leads, one who knew the application in and out, and one who was there to integrate industrialized solutions and optimize the security.

All the meeting rooms at our client's building had zero direct sunlight. There were windows, but they only gave a view of the hallway. Since nobody liked feeling like a goldfish during their meetings, everybody kept the stores shut during meetings, giving the place the feeling of a bunker. Posters covered the walls, but they were all to do with work—Agile methodology, the importance of Quality Assurance, technical posters—so they hardly helped to lighten the mood.

Luckily, the client seemed like a nice guy. He looked to be in his mid-fifties, with graying short hair, the body of someone who worked out regularly, and a ready smile. His suit looked tailored, but he'd opted out of the tie and left the top button of his white shirt open. He followed the unwritten dress rules and liked quality clothes but kept it relatively casual.

The four of us—two Project Managers and two Tech Leads—trooped into the room with Olivier leading the charge. He would make all the introductions, explain my presence and his departure, then leave me to handle the rest of the meeting. I was a little nervous, but no more than expected. Once I started talking, I'd be fine.

While Olivier did his speech, my eyes kept being drawn in Fidi's direction. I blamed the shirt. Where the rest of us wore the most neutral colors in the book—white, black, gray, and a very dark blue for my shirt—Fidi had chosen a Fuchsia shirt. Fuchsia. Even I wasn't going to call it pink because this was as far from the soft pastel color as you could get.

It should have been gaudy. Or ugly. Or some other negative word.

But it wasn't. It made his dark skin look luminous and alive. It made the bunker-like room a little more bearable. It made me want to follow him around like a puppy to see what kind of fun stuff he'd do.

Of course, it also made him look gay as hell, but we'd already established that that wasn't a problem for Fidi.

"Tristan," Olivier said, snapping me back to the conversation. "Why don't you take over from here?"

I cleared my throat. "Thank you, Olivier." Thanking whichever god might be listening that we'd prepared this meeting in detail, so it wasn't a big deal if I hadn't heard a word of what Olivier had said, I launched into my part of the meeting. I gave my credentials on past projects, lying through my teeth when I explained that we'd been working toward my second-in-command taking over for a while, and enthused over the opportunity I thought taking over this project was.

The client seemed to buy it, so my acting skills must have improved considerably since middle school.

Next up was Fidi doing his spiel.

I sat spellbound as he explained his resume, using his entire body as a prop. His hands animated everything, indicating the size of a project or how long ago it was, making *who knows?* gestures when talking about a client who spent millions on an application that would be outdated almost immediately, giving thumbs up to a project that had been expertly managed. And jazz hands. The guy actually pulled off using jazz hands to ironically paint himself as the guy working magic on an application to improve performance or security.

Throughout, he put extra weight on all his experience within Application Security in the hopes that this would explain why we suddenly had a position almost exclusively focused on the subject.

The client seemed to buy it. I could also see him eying Fidi's shirt and when the arm-flapping was at a maximum, a tiny frown line appeared between his eyebrows, but he nodded along where appropriate and asked a couple of questions about a past project in Paris that he seemed to know about.

When Fidi was finished, the client, Monsieur Houliez, addressed Fidi as he folded his hands on the table. "So, what is the security status of our application?"

Fidi flashed a smile. "That's what I'm here to figure out, Monsieur Houliez. I've already started the work, of course, but I prefer to make a complete go-through before giving you the status quo."

Monsieur Houliez seemed to accept this answer, though he clearly wanted more from Fidi.

Luckily, Fidi understood, and launched into a detailed explanation of everything that we could do to improve application security, claiming some things were already in place—he'd spent enough time studying the code to know where he could get away with lying or fudging the dates—and selling the stuff that wasn't yet implemented but would be soon, as nice-to-have features even if most of them were closer to essential.

Monsieur Houliez bought it. I'd even go so far as to claim he got carried away a little on Fidi's enthusiasm.

I certainly did. I was thoroughly impressed with how he threw his entire body into what he said and how clearly passionate he was about his job. The guy knew his stuff, even more than what

I'd picked up on over the last two weeks, which meant that he was humble and let his work speak for itself.

Fifteen minutes later, as we exchanged our visitors' badges for our identity cards at the guardhouse, Olivier met my gaze. "Well, I think that went pretty well, don't you?"

"Yes," I agreed. "It did. I'd say we've convinced him there's nothing suspicious about the two of us showing up right now. He's even happy that we're putting so much effort into the different security measures."

"Now we just have to implement three months' worth of work in about a third of the time," Fidi said, a fake manic smile stretching across his pretty face. "And…some other stuff." He'd just realized that Denis was standing with us, and he wasn't in the know concerning the security breach.

Denis didn't seem to notice how Fidi had just drifted off. In fact, all his attention seemed to be on his phone as he tapped on his screen at lightning speed, a small smile tugging at the corners of his mouth.

"All right." I clapped my hands briskly. "What do you say we eat together at that Chinese restaurant just down the street to celebrate the non-catastrophic outcome of the meeting? I hear it's pretty good."

"Sure," Olivier said before giving Fidi a pointed look. "So long as a certain someone promises there will be no touching."

Fidi rolled his eyes. "Don't worry, big guy. I won't touch you ever again. And anyway, you're not my type."

I couldn't help but wonder what his type was and almost jumped out of my skin when I heard the question voiced, worried I'd said it out loud.

But no, it was Denis of all people, his phone out of sight for once and a genuinely curious look in his eyes as he addressed Fidi.

"Sorry. That's confidential information," Fidi quipped, followed by a short laugh.

But I could have sworn that before he turned away to walk toward his car, a blush had crept into his cheeks.

NINE

Bring It On, Straight Boy

Friday night found the entire team gathered in the company's parking lot. Everybody had managed to free up their weekend—not surprising, considering most of them were single and we were offering them a free weekend of hiking and eating in the Pyrenees. It had been too last-minute to hire a bus, but four of us were more than willing to use our own cars for the hour-long drive.

I took Fidi, Laure, and Denis with me. Without a word, Denis and Laure got in the back, leaving Fidi to ride shotgun.

Fidi hadn't tried anything new since the day I pulled him into my lap. For a day or two, I hoped he'd finished his little game, but the contemplative stares he kept sending in my direction made me suspect he was just planning his revenge.

News of our little encounter had quickly made the tour of the team. I'm not sure what the girls thought, but the guys certainly took great satisfaction in seeing me getting the better of their tormentor. Henri, one of the developers who'd been on the team for close to two years, even went so far as to thank me for sacrificing myself for the greater good.

None of the guys' behavior bothered me in the least. I really didn't think they were homophobic—or I would've noticed by now with Fidi on the team—but they'd been put in a weird position by their new Tech Lead, and somehow now saw me as their Savior.

Without intending to do so, Fidi had helped me big-time to get into the good graces of our new team.

Fidi being Fidi, he'd also found his spot, weird behavior notwithstanding. It was impossible not to like him.

"So," Fidi said as I pulled out of the parking lot and followed my phone's directions toward the A64 highway. "You still up for sharing a room this weekend? From what I can understand of the descriptions, we have a bunch of doubles."

"Of course I'm still up for it," I replied. "Did you actually think I'd back out?"

Out of the corner of my eye, I could see Fidi settling in against the door so he could look at me without giving himself a kink in his neck. It was frustrating not being able to stare right back, but I also very much enjoyed the attention. Tingles of warmth shot up my arms and neck.

"No," he said, his voice contemplative, "I didn't." He flashed that smile of his, visible even in my peripheral vision. "Just making sure I'll have my fun this weekend."

I snorted a laugh. I was suddenly very glad that Fidi had his ridiculous game going on, because it actually allowed me to flirt with my crush with minimal risk of discovery.

"Who's to say you're the only one who'll have fun?"

That smile again. "Oh, that's how it's going to be, huh? All right, bring it on, straight boy."

If I had been straight, I would indeed have been playing a losing game. In fact, even a gay guy who wasn't attracted to Fidi would be playing a losing game. Clearly, Fidi didn't mind getting close, and no matter what your sexual orientation, someone you're not attracted to getting too close was going to make you step away eventually.

At some point, I'd have to have a serious talk with Fidi about this game of his, or he'd find himself in trouble someday. But that talk could wait a few more days.

First, I was going to play. And I played to win.

I glanced in the rearview mirror to see what Laure and Denis were up to. They'd been completely silent since we started, making me almost forget their presence altogether. They were both hunkered over their phones, necks bent and fingers flying over the screens at a speed only possible for a generation who'd gotten their first smartphones before they could even vote.

I considered trying to strike up a conversation which could include the both of them, but they seemed happy with whatever they were doing, Laure flashing a smile as I looked at her and Denis sporting a blush, so I left them to it.

We drove in silence for five minutes, with only the lady on my phone interrupting from time to time to give me directions. I followed them diligently while searching desperately for a conversation topic. How could it be so hard to find something innocent to talk about?

"So you're from the Albi office, huh?" I ended up blurting out.

A pause, where I was certain Fidi was making fun of me for my choice of topic.

"Yup," he finally said. "Been working there for the past three years."

"Where are you staying in Toulouse?"

Fidi lifted one shoulder in a shrug. "Don't have a place here. I take the train back and forth every day."

"Shit," I said, eloquent as always. "That's like an hour each way."

"Mmm." He turned to glance at a truck we were overtaking. "More, actually, since the office isn't exactly in the city center."

"Why don't you get a place closer to work?"

"Because I happen to like my flat." The *you idiot* was silent, but I heard it anyway. "And I don't know how long I'll be here for. So, for the time being, at least, I'll take the commute."

I frowned at the windshield. "You're not staying?" Since me taking over as Project Manager was clearly a permanent thing, I'd assumed it was the same for Fidi.

He just shrugged again. "Probably not in the long run." He glanced in Denis' direction in the backseat, but Denis wasn't listening. He'd gone so far as to plug in his earphones, so we could probably trash talk him as much as we wanted and he wouldn't notice. "Denis is more than capable of doing the work once I get him up to speed on all the security stuff. There's really no need for two Tech Leads on a project like this."

And there was no way someone as talented as Fidi would stay on the project as a simple developer.

I swallowed my disappointment and reminded myself that we were far from being out of the woods with our security breach, so Fidi would be with us for a while.

I vowed to take advantage of his presence while I still could and launched into a monologue on the latest fantasy books I'd read. I didn't usually share much about myself at work, probably my resistance on the gay issue leaking into all other aspects of my life, so I was too nervous to even look at Fidi to gauge his reaction. I did get the occasional comment or question, though, so he didn't seem to find my tastes in books too geeky.

When I ran out of steam, he even took over the conversation. Turned out, he loved gaming, especially strategic games like *Civilization*, or the occasional first-person shooter game when he was feeling especially frustrated.

The GPS woman telling me we had arrived at our destination had me make a double take. Had it really already been an hour and a half?

There was a slight chance my crush was a little more severe than usual.

TEN

Sharing With the Gay Guy

"There are two rooms with double beds." Mathieu stood halfway down the stairs in the cottage we'd rented for the weekend, with his arms crossed and his dark brows drawn together in a frown. "I'm not sharing a double with Denis."

"I'm sure that won't be necessary," I told him as I deposited my backpack on the pile of bags next to the door.

The cottage seemed really nice, with a large living room housing two large sofas turned toward an open fireplace, an equally large kitchen with all types of appliances, and at least three bathrooms, something that would come in real handy when eleven people would need to get ready in the morning. There were five bedrooms, one of which was a triple, and two of which, apparently, housed double beds instead of twins.

Laure adjusted her barrette—the pink one, which seemed to be a favorite. "I don't mind sharing a bed with Sylvie."

With only two women on the team, the decision of who they would share a room with had been the day's easiest decision.

"That's fine with me, too," Sylvie said from the couch, where the tall blonde woman had already made herself comfortable with what appeared to be knitting. "I sleep like the dead anyway."

Mathieu still occupied the staircase, showing off his muscles. He might not have much volume, but I would not want to face him in a fight.

"That still leaves one double," Mathieu said. The man had softened toward me somewhat since the first day, especially after I'd gotten the best of Fidi, but he was far from my biggest fan. I felt his gaze follow me whenever we were in the same room, searching for errors or weaknesses. I sincerely hoped he'd get over his jealousy soon, or I might have to ask Dimitri to move him to a different team. I couldn't risk him undermining my work in any way.

"Fidi and I can take the other one," I told him, schooling my features to hold back an eye-roll. *This* was typical straight guy bullshit. As if it would kill them to share a bed for two nights. As long as neither of them was interested in the other, what did they expect would happen, exactly? Especially a guy like Mathieu, who should be able to thwart any advances from geeky Denis with one arm, probably in his sleep.

Fidi's head snapped toward me, his eyes wide.

Didn't expect that, did you? Yeah, Fidi might be in for a few surprises this weekend.

"You don't mind, do you?" I said sweetly, batting my eyelashes at him.

Mathieu's frown deepened, Denis blushed, and Laure and Sylvie burst out laughing. Team building well on the way.

Recovering quickly, Fidi batted his eyelashes right back at me, and added in that stunning smile of his, making my knees go weak.

"Oh, I don't mind," he crooned. "At. All."

"Excellent." I was happy to discover my voice sounded normal. "Mathieu, where is this double room? I'll drop my bag in there straight away."

Mathieu pointed to the first door on the left at the top of the stairs, and I grabbed my backpack from the pile and hurried past him.

Hoping for even a queen-sized bed would probably have been optimistic, but I still swallowed at the sight of where I'd be spending the next two nights. It was the type of bed you found in most French hotels, where there was technically room for two, but even actual couples found them a tight fit. Sharing it with Fidi was going to be…interesting.

At least neither of us was built like Olivier. Right. Think positive.

"This certainly looks cozy." Fidi squeezed into the room behind me, his suitcase—black and pink like some sort of flashy zebra—behind him. He gave me a questioning look. "Which side of the bed do you sleep on?"

I dumped my backpack on the right side of the bed. "This one."

"Fair enough." Fidi shoved his suitcase into the corner on the left side. "I usually sleep in the middle, so—"

"You're not sleeping in the middle tonight," I warned him, and I was embarrassed to hear a small growl escape me.

Fidi just waggled his eyebrows at me. "We'll see."

Gritting my teeth to fight the arousal I felt at the idea of Fidi sleeping stretched across my body, I forced myself to walk out of the room. "No need to worry about that now, anyway. It's already seven thirty and we need to fix dinner for eleven people."

"Sure, *chef*," he said, following right behind me. "I'll let you decide how to put me to good use. I'm really good with my hands."

"Dear lord," I whispered to myself.

ELEVEN

Nobody Bests Me at This Game

Downstairs, we found seven guys in the kitchen and the two girls lounging on the couch.

"We're doing the dishes after," Sylvie informed me, her eyes on her knitting.

"Sounds fair," I said. I rubbed my hands and asked the group, "Where do you want me?"

I was greeted with silence and my team looking to each other for someone to step forward.

"Seriously?" I asked with a smile. "You guys all looked so busy right now. Do you at least know what we're having tonight?"

"Beer?" Mathieu offered me a bottle.

"Or Pastis," Denis offered from the back.

I shook my head but kept smiling to show them this was okay. "I know we said alcohol would be tolerated, but you do realize it's not a food group, right?"

Fidi reached past me to grab the beer from Mathieu. "There are so many calories in these things, I'm pretty sure we wouldn't starve if that's all we had all weekend." He expertly popped the cap on the kitchen counter and took a sip.

I tracked the movement of the bottle, the way his lips parted to drink, and the movement of his Adam's apple when he swallowed.

"We'd need more than three bathrooms, though," Laure called out from the couch. "We have everything you need to make lasagna." She eyed the lot of us for a moment before adding, "I'm hungry."

Denis held up his phone. "I've got the recipe for lasagna!"

"Excellent," I said and grabbed a beer from the stash filling the entire bottom half of the fridge. There were many of us, but we might have overdone it just a little on the shopping.

I squared my shoulders and faced my team. "I want two people cutting carrots and whatever other vegetables we're supposed to put in the lasagna, two on frying the onions and the meat, one on the béchamel sauce. Uh…" I floundered. Setting nine people to prepare dinner was kind of an overkill.

"Denis can clean the salad," Fidi said. "Olivier can set the table. And you and me can take care of the dressing."

"Right." I nodded decisively. "Sounds like a plan."

And so, we set to it, each team selecting a section of the kitchen to do their work. The vegetable-cutting team took up the largest of the counters and the onion-and-meat and béchamel teams occupied the stove. Denis set up at the sink—which left Fidi and me with the very edge of a counter to prepare the dressing.

Setting aside his beer, Fidi bent to rummage through the bags of groceries at his feet. "Olive oil." A tanned arm came up to set the oil on the counter. "Salt. Pepper. Balsamic vinegar." He straightened and flashed a smile. "Did you get a good look?"

I frowned. "A good look?"

"At my ass." His smile went wider than I'd ever seen it. "When I bent down. You were totally checking me out, weren't you?"

I *had* been checking him out, of course. But knowing this was all a game to him, to scare the straight guy, I didn't even blush as I replied, "Well, I should know what I'm going to bed with. Fair's fair."

I heard a choking noise behind me. I was fairly certain it was one of the guys laughing. In various ways, they'd all made clear to me over the past week that they admired how I handled Fidi and his odd ways. They really wanted me to get the best of him.

And I would do my utmost to satisfy them.

Fidi threw back his head and laughed. The muscles of his neck stood out, making me want to trace them with my tongue.

Suddenly serious, he stepped closer. He wasn't touching me in any way, but I could feel his body heat all down my side. "You might want to check out more details. If we're to share a bed and all." He cocked his head to the side and leaned in, his neck so close to my face I could have touched his Adam's apple by flicking out my tongue.

He smelled delicious. Soap and warm skin, with a hint of the ocean. I could imagine myself spending hours just nuzzling his neck, getting to know the muscles, the beat of his pulse, the angle of his spine. It smelled safe, and new, and pretty.

I hummed as I shifted just a fraction. Not so that there would be any skin-on-skin contact, but so that my breath would brush against the tender skin behind his ear.

"You'll do," I said.

None of the others would have seen it, but since Fidi was literally in my face, I caught his shiver at my words and I bit back a victorious grin.

He rocked back on his heels far enough to meet my eyes. "Seriously, dude," he said, his voice in a slightly higher register than normal. "Don't you have any limits?"

I scoffed. "You're one to talk." I shoved my index into his chest, ignoring my brain telling me this was the first physical contact of the evening. "Let me turn it around for you, Fidi. How far are you willing to go for your game? What if you go up against a guy who'll never stop you? Will you touch him? Kiss him? Even more?"

The kitchen had gone silent, only the clicking of Sylvie's needles keeping us from hearing the proverbial pin drop.

"How far will you go, Fidi? Where's *your* limit?"

Fidi met my gaze and held it for what felt like an eternity. I wasn't entirely certain he was actually seeing me, he seemed to be churning my words over. I wondered if I might actually have gotten through to him.

Finally, he shrugged back online. A second later, the smile was back in full wattage and he offered me a wink. "Well, if I tell you that, it'll ruin the game. You're a worthy opponent, Tristan, I'll give you that. But nobody bests me at this game. Nobody."

I wondered how he'd managed to play this "game" of his for so long, and only just now have ended up against a gay guy, someone who didn't mind the nearness of another man.

But as I could confirm myself, any gay men in our company were closeted. So it was possible—in fact, highly probable—that if he'd tried this on any of them, they would have run for the hills even sooner than the straight guys.

Was that what I should have done?

The thought sped off as Fidi came close enough to smell again. "Enough flirting. We need to rock this dressing."

Who cared what I should have done. I was having fun, and I intended to enjoy this weekend with my team. And my crush.

TWELVE

We'll Do It Outside

I ONCE AGAIN ended up seated next to Fidi and Olivier, across from Laure, Denis, and Sylvie. It seemed like we all naturally flocked together with the people we shared an office with, and the team was divided into two different offices. I vowed to spend some time with the other half of the team later in the evening—I had to get to know them all if I was to have any chance of identifying who our culprit was.

Fidi clearly also remembered the main goal for the weekend and struck up a conversation with Denis on the intricacies of writing secure code. Laure seemed to follow the conversation, though she never contributed anything.

Denis seemed to know what he was talking about. He'd attended all of our company's trainings on application security, seemed to have been reading up on it in his spare time, and had been on a project with strict security needs and measures before he was hired with us. He gestured while he talked, proving how passionate he was about the subject, almost throwing lasagna on Laure's lap on one occasion, making him blush so hard I worried he wouldn't have any blood left for the rest of his body.

It made me wonder how it was possible for us to have such a low level of security if our Tech Lead knew so much about the subject.

Fidi seemed agree with me. "Denis," he began, then paused while he took a sip of his beer, as if searching for the right words. "All of this stuff you're talking about. Hardly any of it has been implemented in the code for our project."

Denis seemed to have zoned out for a moment, his eyes going wide and a twitch going through his body as if he'd been electrocuted. His hands rested on the edge of the table and his knife slid out of his grip to land on his napkin. "What?" he said, his voice cracking.

Laure adjusted her barrette, her attention on Denis. She seemed to be equally confused by the way he'd checked out. She'd had the same piece of lasagna on her fork for a time now, and half of it fell to her plate, unnoticed. Something told me she wasn't focusing on the non-implemented security issues, but damn if I knew what her deal was.

"How come you haven't taught the team how to write secure code?" Fidi repeated, his pretty face unusually serious. This was the Fidi who'd made a name for himself in the workplace, who knew his job and how to get things done. He'd placed his fork and knife on his empty plate, handles pointing right, like you're supposed to in a restaurant, to indicate you've finished eating. His back was straight, his lips set in a firm line, and his arms loosely crossed on the table in front of him.

My crush was getting worse by the second. If he didn't show any faults soon, I might be in trouble.

Denis came back to us and ran a hand through his thinning hair. "Sorry. I couldn't remember if I'd locked the door to my flat before I left. But I did."

We all frowned at that explanation, but none of us called him on it.

"Secure code." Denis's gaze flicked from Fidi, to me, to Olivier. He licked his lips and ran a hand through his hair a second time. "I've done what I could while following the instructions I was given. I was told the developers were supposed to already know how to write clean code, and that we didn't have the time or resources at the moment to set up a tool to do the checks daily."

Ah. A good Tech Lead would have found a way to check the work of the team anyway, but his work would be made a lot more difficult if he didn't have the PM backing him.

I turned to Olivier, doing my best not to sound accusing. "I thought we'd told the client that we'd be doing all that stuff for the next delivery?" I was fairly certain I sounded curious, as if not understanding the discrepancies between my two sources of information.

Though he'd just had a second helping, Olivier put his fork down and leaned back in his chair to cross his arms, showing off all his muscle.

Too bad for him I wasn't into that amount of muscle, and I couldn't help but notice that Fidi didn't appear impressed, either.

"We *were* going to do it," Olivier said. "We just hadn't gotten around to it yet. Delivery isn't for another couple of months."

"True." Fidi raised his eyebrows at Olivier. "But this isn't the type of thing we do just to pretend to the client that we've done it. It's there for a reason. Actually." He turned to me. "Do you know if everybody's had an awareness session on security issues? Everybody's supposed to get that when they're hired, right?"

"Supposedly," I agreed. "But I can't guarantee it's always done."

I noticed Laure frowning, so I asked her if she'd attended the awareness session.

"I don't know," she said, her eyes wide. I'd noticed she didn't like having the attention of too many people at once, and now she had all three of us staring her down. "There were some presentations the first day, but I don't really remember much of it."

Tsking, Fidi shook his head. "That's just general information on the day-to-day workings of the company." He hung his head, drew a deep breath, and straightened again. He met my eyes. "So basically, there's a good chance that the team hasn't even had the spiel on what not to do with client data and external USB drives, and the basic security risks that we might be facing."

I bit back a sigh. "Guess so." It kept getting less and less surprising that we'd had a security breach in the first place.

I knew this wasn't going to make me popular, but I had a job to do, and this weekend was being paid by the company so that we'd save face with the client. "Fidi, I'm guessing you know the content of that awareness session inside out?"

Narrowing his eyes at me, he nodded.

"How about you give it to the team sometime next week? Monday morning?"

Fidi raised a brow and his lips curled into a skeptical frown. "Where would we do it? It's impossible to get meeting rooms on such short notice."

"We don't need a classroom or anything. We just need to be able to hear you. We can do it outside."

He flashed that gorgeous smile again. His voice dropped an octave as his voice turned suggestive. "Oh, I'd love to do it outside."

I tried, but failed, to bite back a laugh, so ended up sounding like I was choking. "Seriously," I whispered as my eyes watered. I cleared my throat, forcing on a serious face. "Okay then. We'll do the security awareness Monday. Outside."

Fidi eyed me while he finished off his beer. "You're no fun," he complained.

But I could tell he was also fighting back a smile.

THIRTEEN

Will You Back Down?

I SPENT THE second part of the evening—the one where we made a serious dent in the stash of beer—with the guys from my team who I didn't share an office with. I held onto the same bottle of beer all through the night, taking only occasional sips, moving into that strange country where everyone around you is drunk and you're not.

This weekend was still work for me. Two days of Team Building might be good for the group in any case, but I had a mission to accomplish, so there was no way I was getting drunk.

I was happy my team was having fun, though, both because it clearly helped everybody get to know each other and because everybody's tongues loosened with alcohol. If I could get closer to knowing who tried to sell our client's data, that would be awesome.

None of the guys really made any red flags go up, though. Many of them were clueless when it came to simple security measures, but if they were responsible for our breach, it would have been from pure ignorance. There was no way I would discover the culprit by talking to him if that was the case, our answer would come from tracing the actual data. Fidi was on that, I knew, but so far, he'd had no luck in identifying the person selling the data.

Speaking of Fidi…he'd clearly not had any trouble with drinking while on the job. As the evening wore on, he'd become more and more exuberant, talking loudly and animatedly, attempting to kiss Olivier on the cheek, and sharing stories of his exes that you'd normally not hear in the workplace.

The team reacted with a mix of fascination, love, and unease. Luckily, the latter was rare, and I had a feeling that although he wouldn't be making any headway on our security issue, at least the team was becoming more comfortable with his attraction to men. Denis especially showed a definite interest in one of the stories, where Fidi had been involved with a guy who was extremely shy and had used his unorthodox ways to try to get the guy to open up a little.

I couldn't figure out what Fidi's type was. From his anecdotes, I'd say he didn't have one. The only thing they all seemed to have in common was that they were guys. Was it possible to be that open to give just anyone a try?

I certainly had a type, and Fidi checked all the boxes. A little effeminate, but not too much. Fit, but not a mountain of muscles. A good sense of humor and the capacity to make fun of himself. And a very pretty face—though that last point wasn't really on my list, it was just a major bonus when it came to Fidi.

Speaking of which, Fidi flopped down on the couch next to me when Mathieu vacated the seat to get ready for bed.

"Ready for bed, handsome?" He leered at me.

"You certainly are," I replied. "Is there any alcohol left for tomorrow night?"

Fidi kept a goofy smile on his face as he watched our colleagues move around us, cleaning up the empty bottles and drying off the last dishes. "I wouldn't know," he said when nobody else was within earshot. "I haven't had more than the one beer."

My head snapped toward him in surprise. His eyes looked normal, their usual onyx beautiful selves, and a lazy smiled played across his lips.

"Seems my performance is Oscar-worthy, huh?" He winked. "We have a job to do, Tristan. I'm not about to get drunk off my ass in this context." His gaze turned inward and a wistful smile appeared. "I get way too chatty when I'm drunk. Wouldn't want to divulge any company secrets."

"That would be best, yes," I agreed. "I'm impressed," I admitted. "I was convinced you'd downed more beer than the rest of the team combined. You certainly had the chatty bit down pat."

Fidi waggled his eyebrows at me. With a theatrical sigh, he lurched into a standing position, still in character. "I'm off to bed. You coming?"

I saw an opportunity and jumped at it. "Why don't I help you up the stairs." I stood and folded his arm across my shoulders before slipping mine around his waist. "Wouldn't want the drunk Tech Lead to fall down the stairs."

"How thoughtful of you."

His face was so close to mine in this position, I didn't dare meet his eyes. I had enough reveling in the feel of his body next to mine, his body heat sending shivers up my arm and my side, and the scent of citrus and healthy male filling my nostrils.

We made our way to our room. When we met Olivier at the bottom of the stairs, he rolled his eyes at Fidi, clearly suspecting that he'd forced me to half-carry him up the stairs as part of his game. Denis's eyes were for me, shining with appreciation, though I wasn't sure if it was for taking Fidi off their backs or just for taking care of a drunk colleague.

We took our turns in the collective bathroom, and finally, found ourselves alone in our bedroom.

With its tiny bed.

"So, did you find out anything interesting tonight?" I asked to stop obsessing with our sleeping arrangements. I started unbuttoning my shirt and sent my sneakers flying into the corner.

"Kind of," Fidi replied. He was making short work of his own shirt, deft fingers slipping the buttons free, his coordination back to stellar now that the rest of the team wasn't around to observe.

I considered the possibility of turning my back to give us both some privacy, but *he* wasn't turning away. I wasn't about to let him see I was uncomfortable—and I didn't want to miss the show.

Fidi talked as he shrugged out of his shirt, pulling on the cuffs to fit them over his hands. "The stupid ones are so stupid that if they were at the source of our security breach, it's done entirely on accident, and they've done nothing to hide the traces. It means we'll probably figure out who it was if I ever manage to put my hands on the database."

He folded his shirt neatly and draped it over his bag on the floor, then started unbuttoning his jeans.

I couldn't have turned away if I'd wanted to. And the best part was that Fidi seemed completely oblivious that I was ogling him. I was so firmly in his "straight" box, he wasn't even looking for signs. I started in on my own pants, trying to remember the finer details of my Automation classes, a trick that usually worked when I didn't want to tent my boxers.

"I have a short-list of main suspects," Fidi continued. "Several people on the team could have done it and have some sort of motive. Olivier, Mathieu, Denis, and Laure are all on the list, obviously."

I nodded as I threw my jeans on top of my shirt, deciding that would be this weekend's dirty clothes heap. "And how are you doing on catching up to the database?"

Fidi placed his neatly folded jeans on top of his shirt and proceeded to remove his socks, bundle them together, and toss them on top of the pile. "I'm getting there. I'm in contact with the person selling and am asking a lot of questions on the data, ostensibly to check their veracity, but I'm hoping whoever I'm talking to will end up giving himself away in some way or another.

We were both down to our boxers. I refrained from looking too closely because his were tight-fitting and *pink* and I was having a hard enough time not showing anything in my looser, black version as it was. I couldn't look him in the face and not notice that his chest was smooth, though. Even on his legs, he seemed to have only sparse body hair.

I felt like a bear in comparison, but the way Fidi's eyes kept darting down to my chest was promising.

Suddenly, the calculating gleam was back in his eyes and he took a step toward me. "So, *chef*. Still sure you're up to sharing a bed with the gay guy?"

"I said I was, didn't I?" My entire body was lighting up as I, again, caught Fidi's citrus scent and I couldn't decide if I should run away or step closer. I ended up doing neither.

"That's a very small bed," he said, his eyes on mine, searching for a reaction. "We'll be really close. Kind of like this."

He stepped so close I could feel his body heat, but there was still no skin-to-skin contact.

I cocked my head, praying I could keep my voice even. I needed to play this cool. "I told you I don't like losing."

His eyes narrowed. "So you're just never going to back down? No matter what I do? I find that hard to believe."

I had something else that was turning hard, so I needed to end this confrontation pronto.

Without really thinking things through, I leaned closer, so close our lips were millimeters from touching. "What about you?" I whispered. "Will you never back down? Even if I do this?"

And I leaned in and kissed him.

His lips were as soft as they looked, and it felt like I could plunge safely into them and disappear into their depths forever.

My eyes slid shut of their own accord, but I forced them open and ended the kiss as quickly as it had begun.

Fidi stood frozen, his eyes wide. I wasn't entirely certain he was breathing.

"I'm going to turn in," I told him and jumped into the bed, taking care to hide the front of my boxers. Once I was safely under the covers, I met his gaze again. "Are you coming? Or were you planning on sleeping on the floor?"

When he still didn't move, I said, "I'm turning off the light, all right? Good night." I reached out to flip the switch next to the bed and plunged the room into darkness.

FOURTEEN

Soft Colors and Handsome Princes

I WOKE UP feeling warm and safe. My face was full of smooth skin, as was the entire front of my body. I vaguely realized that I was snuggling up to Fidi, but just couldn't bring myself to care enough to move away. The smell of his skin and heat of his body were just too damn nice.

Even through my closed eyelids I could see the sunlight streaming into the room—we'd forgotten to close the blinds before going to bed last night. It made the whole experience feel like a fairy tale with soft colors and handsome princes.

I furrowed my nose into what must be Fidi's neck, and my hips moved of their own accord to get closer to his leg. The friction was heavenly.

I did it again.

Movement under my chin. I must have been lying in the crook of his arm and that smooth skin against my scruff was Fidi's bicep.

I hummed in satisfaction and flexed my hips again.

"Tristan?" Fidi's voice was gruff as he spoke right into my ear, making me shiver.

"Mmm."

"Are you awake? You do realize you're dry-humping my leg? And that your knee is touching my balls?" His voice was oddly neutral. I couldn't quite decide if he was annoyed or amused.

Also, I wasn't awake enough to care. I hummed again and stretched to get a good sniff of the spot where his neck met his shoulders. I'd always been a sucker for latching onto a man's neck.

Fidi let out a shaky sigh which turned into a hiss when I gave his balls a nudge with my knee and flexed my hips again for good measure.

"You're gay, aren't you?" he said, defeat lacing his voice. I felt him melt into the mattress beneath us as tension left his muscles.

"Mmm." I extended my tongue to lick at the little hollow above his breastbone. "Took you long enough to catch on. I was wondering if I'd have to fuck you before you figured it out." I humped his leg again, partly to underline my point, and partly because I didn't have it in me to stop. "Not that I'd really mind."

Fidi whimpered. I felt an aborted movement under the leg I had draped over him—I was guessing he was also searching for friction.

I finally opened my eyes.

I had the covers drawn up to my ears and Fidi filled my entire line of vision. His smooth, tanned chest was spread out before me and dark eyes peered down at me from beneath a wild bed-head. I was kind of relieved to discover that he didn't wake up perfectly coiffed.

"Morning," I said. When I didn't get a reply, I added, "You say the word and I'll stop dry-humping your leg, promise."

His eyes kept searching my face. "You're really awake?"

I moved my hips again, with more force this time, so that he couldn't miss how hard I was. "What do you think?" Then I groaned into his neck. It had been too long since my dick had had any kind of human contact outside of my own hand.

Finally, he got the memo. "Fuck it," he muttered, before putting his free hand to my jaw and drawing me up to kiss him.

His lips were just as soft as the night before. And now that he was kissing me back, I could fall into them completely and drown in soft bliss.

I licked quickly at his lips, asking for entrance, and he allowed me in on a soft moan. Everything escalated from there. Our tongues tangled as I moved farther up on the bed, both to deepen the kiss and to get the interesting bits farther South to align.

He put his hands in my hair, pulling on the strands and massaging my scalp.

My right hand caressed his neck, while the left started fumbling with the elastic of my boxers. I made quick work of my own, but Fidi's tight-fitting version was more complicated.

I broke the kiss and leaned back so I could use both hands.

Fidi lay sprawled out on the bed, the slanting sunlight reflecting off the highlights in his hair and his tanned chest heaving with rapid breaths.

"This is probably a bad idea," he said as he lifted his hips to make my work easier.

"You're probably right," I replied and sent his pink boxers flying.

I resumed my position on top of him and latched my lips to his again. I'd never felt such softness before and had to get as much as possible while I had the chance. We both let out low moans as our bodies aligned, this time with no clothing in the way. Fidi was giving off heat like a furnace and I just wanted to crawl right into him and stake my claim.

As his hands resumed pulling on my hair, tilting my head at the angle he wanted, I let my hand crawl down between our bodies, where our dicks were already trying to figure out how to dance. I figured I'd help them along and took us both in hand.

I couldn't fit my hand completely around the both of us, but it was more than enough to make us both break the kiss and instead moan into each other's mouths.

"We probably shouldn't make too much noise," Fidi said before attacking my mouth again.

I just hummed my agreement. Speech was beyond me at the moment, though I did have enough presence of mind to know I wouldn't want all our coworkers to overhear us having a frottage session in the wee hours of the morning.

Everything sped up; my hand on our dicks, our heartbeats attempting to outrace each other in our chests, the rapid breaths we squeezed in between kisses to avoid passing out from lack of oxygen.

Just as I thought I'd lose face and come before him, Fidi detached from our kiss and threw his head back as he arched his spine. The muscles in his neck corded and his mouth opened in a silent scream.

Seeing a new opportunity, I clamped my mouth down on the juncture of his neck and shoulders—and we went over the cliff together.

"So," Fidi said once we'd had a couple of minutes of silence to catch our breaths. "Gay, huh?"

I chuckled. "No shit, Sherlock."

I was back to lying in the crook of Fidi's neck. Personally, I didn't think I'd want to move for a couple of hours at least. I just wanted to lie here and bask in the afterglow.

Fidi must have had more energy than me; he moved away enough for our eyes to meet, though his arm stayed draped over my shoulder.

"You're in the closet," he said. It wasn't a question.

"Just at work." I shrugged. "I've been out with friends and family since high school."

"But why?" The tiniest of frown lines made an appearance on his forehead. If I hadn't been lying so close, I wouldn't even have seen it.

I started tracing my fingers over his smooth chest, not quite comfortable with meeting his eyes. "Don't want the hassle," I explained. "I wouldn't mind outing myself to my colleagues if I was in a serious relationship, but so long as I'm not, I'd just be fodder for the gossip mill, and I don't see the point."

"So, you're telling me you've never been in a serious relationship?"

I traced a circle around his nipple with my index finger, enjoying seeing it harden at the attention. "Not serious enough, I guess."

I'd had a couple of guys coming close, but each time the relationship had come to an end before I got around to introducing them to my colleagues.

Fidi didn't say anything, but I felt I needed to explain. "Once people know you're gay, that's the first thing that comes to mind when they think about you. It's not the funny guy, or the smart guy, or the annoying dude. It's the gay guy. Hell, even Dimitri did it when he first mentioned you. Your name, he's gay, and oh, by the way, he's a genius with code." I swallowed. "I just don't want to be 'the gay guy' if I don't have to."

Fidi chewed on his bottom lip as he considered. "I guess I can understand that." He brought his hand to mine to stop me from messing with his nipple. "But if we want it to be seen as something normal, *we* have to treat it like it is. It should be as natural as Olivier saying he's into curvaceous women or Mathieu saying he likes them tall and skinny. You like men. So what?"

I heaved a sigh and rolled over to my back, pulling my hand free from his. "I know that, Fidi, believe me. I just don't want to be the gay poster boy at work. I just want to do my job and for people to see that I'm good at it."

"But you'd risk coming out if you met the right guy?" He seemed skeptical.

"Yes." My reply is emphatic. "It's not like it would end my career if people knew I was gay. We live in a free country where gays have the same rights as the straights. It's just…tiring…to always have people's eyes on you, wondering about your sex life." Because I did know those looks. I got them from time to time with certain family members, and quite frequently when I went out with my friends. Nobody had trouble with my sexuality, but that didn't stop them from wondering. And they must not realize that their questions were written on their faces, or they likely would have taken more care.

Fidi extracted his hand and swung his legs over the side of the bed. "I'll believe it when I see it," he said. He bent down to swipe his boxers from the floor and dried off his stomach with them before tossing them into a corner.

"Why, are you volunteering?" I tried for light banter, but must have missed my mark by a mile.

"Not hardly," he replied as he searched through his bag. "I never date closeted guys." He pulled out a large sky-blue towel and hitched it around his waist as he stood up.

The disappointment I felt at his words came as something of a surprise. I kept my voice light as I cleaned myself off with my own boxers. "Then I guess we're at an impasse."

"Guess so. I'm going to take a shower." Without a backward glance, he was out the door.

FIFTEEN

The Show Must Go On

I'D COME OUT to a colleague. And not just any colleague, but an openly gay one with a very clear gay agenda, who would no doubt see it as a victory if a closeted guy came out and stood with him in his fight.

I didn't really think that Fidi would out me, but the worry was eating at me as I sipped my coffee over breakfast.

The team sprawled across the kitchen and living room, with the kitchen counter overflowing with cereals, croissants, bread, and at least five different types of juice.

Fidi was munching on a croissant and holding his mug of coffee close to his chest like it was a dear pet he was afraid would run away if he didn't cuddle it hard enough. His back to the room, he stared out the window, likely admiring the vista of the Pyrenees.

I walked over to stand next to him, my eyes also on the view.

"I know this is an awful cliché," I said, my voice low so nobody would overhear. "But I need to say it anyway. You're not going to tell anyone, right?"

His angry eyes snapped to mine. "Really? You think I'd do that?"

"No," I told him, meeting his eyes. "I really don't. But I also really need to make it clear that I don't want you to tell anyone."

He sighed and went back to staring out the window. "You made that plenty clear earlier. No need to worry."

I sipped my coffee. It was almost cold, but I still needed the caffeine. "Thank you."

There was a racket as Olivier came crashing down the stairs. He must have tripped on one of the last steps and went head-first into the wall next to the foyer.

He emitted an *oof* on impact but bounced back immediately. "I'm fine," he said and held up a hand. The hand moved to his head. "Except...headache. Where's the coffee?"

He seemed to be in an exceptionally good mood for someone with a hangover. In fact, his attitude had slowly changed since the first day we met, from the grumpy, angry rugby player who was losing his project, to a smiling, joking...okay, he was still a rugby player, but the fun sort, who you were never afraid would throw a punch at you for saying the wrong thing.

Sylvie handed him a mug of steaming coffee and Olivier flashed her a brilliant smile.

I had been paying so much attention to Fidi, to his pretty face and the way he kept provoking the team, that I'd totally missed Olivier's real personality. He might have messed up on the security issues at work, but he had the interactions with the rest of the team down pat.

Olivier groaned with pleasure as he downed the first gulp of his coffee. "*Thank you*, Sylvie. You're a life saver."

"Don't thank me," Sylvie said and returned to her seat at the kitchen table. "Thank Fidi. He was the first one out here and has already prepared three batches of that heavenly brew."

Olivier's gaze went to Fidi, then to me standing next to him.

"So you both survived the night, huh?" he asked and winked. "Fidi didn't manage to turn you."

I grinned and turned to Fidi. "And here I thought it was just vampires who couldn't take direct sunlight. The gays are like that, too?"

Fidi chuckled. He drew a hand up as if flicking imaginary hair over his shoulder. "It's a well-known fact that the queens only come out at night."

We all burst out laughing.

Olivier was still staring at us. "So I guess the game's still on then, huh?"

The game? Oh, right, Fidi trying to scare me with his gayness.

I chanced a glance at him. Would he still be doing it now that he knew it would never scare me?

Fidi's nose was buried in his cup, but eventually, he had to come back out.

He flashed a smile that didn't reach his eyes. "If he can take a night sharing a bed with me, I think we're good."

"So I win?" I couldn't decide if this made me happy or not. It should make me happy.

Fidi straightened his back. "I did not say that."

I might have moved closer, because suddenly, my nostrils filled with his citrusy scent again. "If you stop, it means I've won.

You don't get to decide that you suddenly just stop playing. You stop, you forfeit the victory."

I heard Olivier chuckling behind me, but I didn't even turn to look at him.

Fidi chewed on his bottom lip, his eyes searching mine. He was probably wondering if I'd lost my mind.

He might have a point.

I didn't want him to stop. I liked having him in my personal space, and I liked making him flustered.

The game had to continue.

Nobody likes losing at their own game. "The game was to get me to step away from you, and I've never done that. So I win."

Fidi's lips tightened into a firm line. "I've never stepped away from you, either. At best, it's a tie."

I raised my eyebrows. Making sure I had a playful expression on my face, I turned to glance at the team, letting them know I knew they were hanging onto our every word. I waggled my eyebrows.

I turned back to Fidi. "I won't accept a tie. I play to win."

Fidi's frown had taken over his entire face. I felt kind of bad for him, for putting him on the spot like this, but he was getting flustered and my heart was jumping around in my chest doing a little happy dance.

I leaned in and stage-whisper in his ear. "Guess it's my turn to see how close you will let me come."

Olivier roared with laughter, then cut off almost immediately. "Ouch," he complained, both hands holding his head. "Please stop doing funny things until I'm no longer hungover."

Sylvie piped up from her spot on the couch. "I think it's time to open a poll. I say Tristan wins, in…" She cocked her head as she considered. "Two weeks."

Fidi whirled and pointed at her. "I will not hear of any such ridiculous poll."

"It's no more ridiculous than your game," Sylvie pointed out. "But no worries. We'll keep the poll secret. You won't hear a word."

I snorted a laugh and waited for Fidi to turn back to face me.

When he did, I flashed him my best smile. "May the best man win."

SIXTEEN

Beautiful View

My life had a new purpose.

Hiking isn't usually a sport where there's lots of physical contact, but I made do. I had to win the game with Fidi for the sake of the team, and to show him how silly that game of his really was.

At least, that's what I told myself. Really, I was just thrilled to have found an excuse to get close to Fidi any chance I got.

Having a crush had never been so much fun.

The hike we'd chosen wasn't a very long one—we'd correctly anticipated the number of hungover participants who would not want to attempt the higher peaks—but we packed a picnic. Everybody carried a small backpack with some extra clothing, water, and food, and Olivier took all seven boxes of pâté. As he tore up the slope ahead of the group, looking like an overly muscled version of a gazelle, I suspected we should also have given him all the water.

We walked in a line, and I made sure to get the spot behind Fidi.

It was the first time I saw him in shorts—though I guess the same went for all the guys on the team since one of the only rules for clothing in the office was that the guys wear pants—and I couldn't tear my eyes away from his ass and legs.

At first, I just enjoyed the view. The turquoise athletic shorts hugged his body perfectly. I had an unimpeded view of his thighs pumping and ass moving with every step, and since the mountain was kind enough to be rather steep, all of this was right in my line of vision coming up behind him.

But I had a game to win. I made sure Denis was close enough behind me to overhear, then said, "Man, the view is really spectacular."

"Sure is," Denis replied. His voice was a little distant because he had—as you would—turned around to admire the view behind us.

Fidi turned to do the same. He frowned when he saw me with my back to the hills and plains below us.

"The view's that way," he said.

I grinned. "Okay." I let my gaze drop to his shorts.

He snorted. "Smooth."

"Oh, I wasn't aiming for smooth. I enjoy a more direct approach." I was studying his legs. The muscles of a runner, and hardly any body hair. I wanted to run my hands down his calves to see if maybe he had some hair that wasn't visible from afar.

"Are you guys discussing what I think you're discussing?" Laure had caught up to Denis and stopped behind him on the path. Today's barrette was a white flower, a lily if I wasn't mistaken.

"If you mean my ass," Fidi said, hands on hips and an exasperated sigh on his voice. "Then yes, we are. Apparently."

"Oh, it's not just your ass," I say, smiling from ear to ear. "Don't sell yourself short, man."

There was silence behind us.

Fidi kept staring at me. His head was shaking, but I didn't think he did it on purpose.

"You know I'll stop if you want me to, right?" I said. "You just say the word, and I'm off you back. And the winner of the game."

Denis whispered to Laure, but I still heard him. "They're still doing that? Isn't this taking being a good sport a bit far?"

Laure giggled. "Let them do their thing. It's fun to watch."

Fidi took a step down so he was on my level and came in close. His face was only a hand's width from mine, within kissing distance.

"It's going to take a lot more than some staring to scare me off, Tristan," he said. He licked his lips and my gaze followed, remembering their softness as we kissed this morning.

"Good," I whispered.

We stood like that for several seconds, neither of us wanting to be the first to back down, even in an insignificant staring match.

"Fidi! Tristan!" Olivier shouted from halfway up the mountain. "What is taking you sissies so long?"

Fidi's eyes shut closed on a sigh. "How can he be so chipper when he's supposed to be hungover?"

"I don't know." I smiled. "But I don't think we should let him get away with calling his boss and Tech Lead sissies. What do you say we team up on him when we reach the lake?"

Fidi's eyes gleamed. "Deal."

SEVENTEEN

Sissies Go for a Swim

OLIVIER MUST HAVE reached the lake a good twenty minutes before us. By the time we caught up with him, he'd set up on the grass by the dreamily turquoise lake, removed his shoes, and stretched out on the grass to take a nap. He was so soundly asleep that we could hear his snoring as we approached and even the chuckles and comments of ten people walking up to him didn't wake him up.

I dumped my backpack next to Olivier's and stood above him, arms crossed as I evaluated the distance from Olivier to the lake.

"Sissies would probably let him have his beauty sleep," I said.

Fidi lined up next to me. "They probably would. But we're not sissies."

"We're not sissies," I agreed. But what could we do? I longed to throw him in the lake, but Olivier really was quite huge, and I doubted that Fidi and I would manage to lift him up, carry him five steps, and then *throw* him in the water. He wouldn't stay still once he woke up. Also, the lake couldn't be more than thirty centimeters deep in the part where we could throw Olivier in, and the bottom was littered with sharp rocks. I didn't want to actually hurt the guy.

Fidi seemed to be doing the same calculations as me. "We could bring the lake to *him*."

The rest of the team were settling in on the bank behind us. They kept a certain distance from the sleeping Olivier. None of them said anything, but their attention was on us, as if we were today's entertainment. From the looks on their faces, we could have asked them to pay to watch and they would have handed over their cash, no questions asked.

I pondered Fidi's proposition. "But how?" I snapped my fingers and started opening my backpack. "The salad bowl. It's huge. Takes up almost my entire backpack."

Chuckling, Fidi helped me pull the large bowl out. "And what do you propose we do with the salad?"

"Everybody." I turned to my team, using my bossy voice, but with minimum volume so as not to wake up our future victim. "Get your plates out. Salad's coming up."

Large grins on their faces, they all followed my order. I would have loved to say it was a testament to my leading skills, but their gleeful anticipation kind of killed that idea.

Three minutes later, everybody had overflowing plates of salads and I had one large, empty salad bowl. I walked some distance down the path by the lake to clean it out, then came back to fill it with clean lake water close to our spot.

"It's freezing," I commented. I was already losing contact with my fingers from the quick wash-up.

"Of course it is," Fidi said. "It's spring and we're in the Pyrenees. This is basically snow that melted very recently."

I eyed the salad bowl, having some second thoughts about our plan of action.

"He'll be fine," Fidi said, dragging me up to stand over Olivier's prone form. "It's close to thirty degrees, he'll dry right up. Unless he's a sissy." He winked at me.

Yeah, couldn't back down from that.

"All right," I said. "Let's do this."

We held the bowl together and moved so we were standing just above Olivier, one on each side.

Olivier kept snoring, his large chest moving up and down and his mouth hanging open.

I met Fidi's gaze and gave him a nod. "Go."

We emptied the bowl on Olivier's chest. The water splashed on his face, down to his shorts, on our legs and shoes, on the grass. It was beautiful.

I started to step away, to get away from whatever Olivier might do, but I was too slow. I hadn't factored in his minimal reaction time or general alertness. Before I could take even one step, he lunged up and grabbed me around the waist.

That was just with one arm. The other had Fidi in a similar grip, and we barely had the time to meet each other's eyes before we were lifted up, carried down to the water, and summarily dumped in.

He must be one hell of a rugby player.

The water was *freezing*.

I didn't even try to hold back my scream and scrambled to get my legs under me. Fidi's voice joined mine. We bumped into each other under the water; my hand on his legs, his head against my shoulder.

Three seconds later we were standing in thirty centimeters of water, soaking wet.

Olivier was in the water with us, but despite the entire salad bowl's worth of water we'd dumped on him, he was dryer than us. Only his front was covered with water, and his shorts were mostly dry, whereas I didn't have a single part of my clothing that was still dry.

"Sissies," Olivier said with a satisfied smile. "I don't know which one of you screamed loudest."

"Fidi," one voice called from the bank, closely followed by another shouting, "Tristan!"

"Both sissies." Olivier's smile was huge, showing a missing molar on one side.

Wrapping both arms around myself, I glanced at Fidi. He was in much the same position, his entire torso already shaking.

"I think we need to admit defeat," I said. "Let's get out of the water." I put my arm around his shoulders and pulled him with me to the shore.

The entire team was roaring with laughter. I wasn't exactly happy with my current situation, but a smile crept across my face anyway. If my team was this entertained, the dunking was probably worth it.

I just needed to make sure neither of us came down with a cold because of our stunt—we didn't have the time for any leave of absence.

"Did you bring any spare clothing?" I asked Fidi. I found my abandoned backpack and searched for the sweater I'd brought.

Fidi's teeth were clattering as he tried using shaking fingers to open his own bag. "I have a windbreaker."

"That'll do." I pulled off my t-shirt and replaced it with the sweater. I felt instantly better, and thankful for the hot sun bearing down on us.

I helped Fidi with his backpack and pulled out his windbreaker. "Take off your shirt," I told him. "Put this on instead."

"Ooh, do you want us to leave?" Mathieu's voice was full of laughter.

"Not now, Mathieu." I kept any reproach out of my voice, but there should be no doubt he'd better listen.

"Sorry, *chef*."

I helped Fidi get out of his soaked t-shirt and quickly wrapped him up in his windbreaker. It was hardly warm, but it was cover, and the sun should help him along in a minute.

My sweater was helping, but my entire lower body was getting colder by the second. I glanced at our audience, and briefly met Laure and Sylvie's eyes. "Will you girls be shocked if I strip down to my boxers?"

"Go ahead," Sylvie said, waving a hand. "Just don't judge us if we admire the view."

Guess I deserved that one.

I stripped out of my shorts, and Fidi did the same next to me. We removed our socks and shoes as well, and I grabbed everything to go hang it to dry on a large boulder down by the water.

When I returned to the group, Fidi had sat down next to Denis, and he'd somehow managed to fit his legs into his windbreaker with his knees to his chest. He wasn't shaking anymore, so I felt confident he'd be okay.

I felt ridiculous standing there with a large sweater that was way too warm for today's weather and no pants. At least my boxers were black and covered everything. I risked a quick glance at Fidi—his boxers were pink. I was surprised nobody had commented on the color, but then again it went with his personality.

I eased down on the grass next to Fidi, stretching my legs out in front of me so they'd soak up as much heat from the sun as possible. "You all right?" I asked him as I bumped my shoulder into his.

"I'll do," he replied. "So that kind of backfired, huh?"

I chuckled. "It was fun. The team enjoyed it." I glanced over to our clothes hanging to dry in the sun. "But I have to admit I'm not looking forward to putting my shorts back on for the return trip."

"You and me both," Fidi said with a shudder.

I put my arm around his shoulder to try to give him some of my warmth and he leaned into my touch.

Denis's voice was low, but I heard him anyway. "Are they still playing that game? I'm confused."

I froze as I realized what I was doing. But I didn't move my hand away. I briefly considered the possibility of leaning in and trying to get a rise out of Fidi, pretending it was all part of the game, but this just wasn't the time. He was cold and miserable, and I wasn't going to add to that.

"The game is on hiatus until we dry up," I said and gave Fidi's shoulder a little squeeze. "Where's my salad?"

EIGHTEEN

Bright Pink Balls

That night, nobody felt like cooking, so we decided to go to a bowling alley in a nearby village and have dinner there.

After a deliciously greasy meal, we created four teams and set ourselves up for a tournament where the losers would be in charge of cleaning the house before we went back to Toulouse and the winners would get to sleep in.

Using our "game" as an excuse, I made sure to be on Fidi's team. We also had Sylvie and Laure, and we played opposite Olivier, Mathieu, Henri, and Denis.

Olivier and Sylvie both took off to search for bowling balls in other stalls; Olivier, because he couldn't find one for hands as big as his, and Sylvie, because her hands were apparently freakishly small.

"Just watch," she told me with a grim scowl as she left. "The ball's going to be bright pink. Hands this small can apparently only belong to cute little girls."

My shoulder brushed against Fidi's as we both searched for bowling balls to our liking. The smell of his shampoo was very faint—a whole day of hiking and a dunk in a mountain lake would do that—but he still smelled of healthy male and I had goosebumps popping up all along my forearms.

"If you don't watch out," Fidi said as he fit three fingers into a midnight blue ball on the rack, "you're going to come tumbling out of the closet if you keep pushing."

I shrugged. "It's your game. I didn't come up with it."

He straightened, hands on his hips. Apparently, he was happy with the midnight blue ball. "And what happens if I keep playing, too? Is there a limit? Or will you still claim it's 'the game' when we make out while waiting for our turn?" He pointed to the seats behind us.

My body was completely on board with that idea.

My head, not so much.

"I don't think you'd do that," I said. A garishly green bowling ball seemed to fit my hand, so I stood tall to face Fidi. "I believe you don't hook up with closeted guys, so you don't want the kissing any more than I do."

Olivier came back and placed a black ball on our rack. The three holes looked like they had room for entire sausages. I'd never realized the guy was *that* big. "You guys ready?" he asked.

We both nodded and retreated to our seats. Everyone except Sylvie had found what they needed, and Denis was going around taking people's orders for a first round.

"All you need to do for me to stop," I whispered to Fidi so nobody would overhear, "is to admit the game is stupid."

"It's not stupid," he mumbles back. "Not when you play it with straight boys."

Clearly, I'd only win by playing this game and giving it one hundred percent. I was okay with that.

I draped an arm across the armrest at Fidi's back and leaned in close enough to see the beginnings of a shadow on his upper lip. Seemed like he couldn't grow a beard even if he wanted to.

"You're a bit slow," I told him, my breath making the hairs on his neck stand up, "if you think I'll let you win. I hope you're not a sore loser."

I saw his jaw work as he ground his teeth, but then he drew a deep breath and his anger seemed to evaporate. A slow smile spread across his delicious lips.

"I've never had a problem with losing," he said. "But I'm also not a quitter." He placed his hand on my thigh.

"Ah. Things are looking up, I see." Sylvie had found what she needed at the very last station—a brightly pink bowling ball, as promised—and plonked it down on our rack before taking a seat next to Fidi. "So, is the game still going?"

I sent her a scowl. "Of course it is. And I'm winning."

Fidi ran a hand down my jaw, scratching his nails against my scruff, making me shudder.

"If you say so, honey," Sylvie said. "If you say so."

NINETEEN

Bowling Technique

Olivier turned out to be a genius with a bowling ball. He threw strike after strike, making me suspect he'd spent as much time in a bowling alley as he had on a rugby field. How he'd found the time to work was beyond me.

Our team was struggling.

Sylvie wasn't too bad. She cleaned out all the kegs at least every other round, and even managed three strikes.

Laure had clearly never held a bowling ball before and hit the gutter more often than she hit the kegs. At first, Olivier tried to give her pointers, but that seemed to make her even more nervous, so Olivier eventually gave up. Denis had better luck, at least with not making her drop the ball on her own feet, though he didn't improve her stats any.

Fidi and I were too busy playing our game to really focus on the bowling.

When he played, I walked up behind him and offered to "help him with his technique." I'm pretty sure he didn't need it, but he never told me to get lost, so I kept at it. I lined up behind him so my chest was to his back, my front pushing up against his ass. When he prepared to launch, I placed my hand on his forearm and pretended to guide his movements.

I got a total kick out of it and had to fight to keep my enthusiasm from tenting my jeans. I lived in a cloud of Fidi-scented bliss.

He hardly hit any kegs, of course. It's kind of hard to bowl well with a guy clinging to your back.

He paid me back by pretending to be the over-the-top gay boyfriend who just couldn't keep himself from complimenting me. He stood by the rack and adopted an unnaturally high and affected voice.

"That's it, *chéri*," he said as I lined up my shot. "Looking good. Show us your ass, now. Yes, just like that!"

That voice must have carried across the entire bowling alley.

The guys from our team were howling with laughter, but the people from the next booth over kept sending us sideways glances and one girl from three or four teams farther down stopped and stared at us when she walked past to go to the bathroom.

Fidi's technique was completely throwing me off my game.

I had one miraculous strike in the very beginning, but from there on out I never managed to down more than four kegs in one round.

Turns out I don't really care about losing when the game's bowling.

We were approaching the end of the game and Fidi had kept a running commentary of my technique for a good five minutes—holding nothing back on the descriptions of the various body parts involved. All our colleagues were clutching their stomachs with laughter, tears streaming down their faces, gasping for air. Basically, the bowling game was completely ignored in favor of our game.

I was enjoying myself immensely. This was working wonders on team morale and I hadn't had this much fun in years. It didn't even matter that it was at my cost.

Fidi also seemed to be having the time of his life. His grin went from ear to ear, his cheeks were flushed, and all his movements were animated, and not just because he was playing into the stereotype.

We both fed off the energy of the group.

After a while, I got used to Fidi's comments, his compliments. I got used to him behaving like my boyfriend.

As I waited my turn, I pondered why I got such a thrill from this. It wasn't new for me to be seen with a guy, for people to know I was gay. I'd had several boyfriends in the past and had introduced them to my friends and family. I couldn't understand why pretending to have a boyfriend should bring me more pleasure than actually having one.

Maybe it was because it was all pretend.

The clock was nearing midnight when we attacked the very last round. We could've stopped half an hour earlier because it was already clear that Olivier would win the game, but none of us were here in search of a big victory.

I was at my usual spot, scotched to Fidi's back as he prepared his last shot, when somebody said my name.

I turned. And froze on the spot.

Christian. My ex.

My two worlds crashed together. This was not good.

I vaguely heard Fidi's ball hitting the kegs. Everybody cheered. "Way to go, Fidi!"

Christian kept looking from me to Fidi to the guys on the team. I could see the thoughts flitting across his pretty face.

I had to interfere before he came to the wrong conclusion.

"Christian!" I walked over to shake his hand. "Imagine meeting you here. Why don't you come say hello to my colleagues. We're here for the weekend." I put just the slightest hint of an accent on the word *colleague* so he'd understand.

The hurt look in his eyes told me he most certainly did.

We'd been together for almost four months when we broke up. I'd been in the process of thinking about coming out at work so that I could introduce my colleagues to my boyfriend, but Christian hadn't thought I'd been quick enough about it. Once he'd started putting pressure on me to tell them, I backtracked and we broke up.

The look he gave Fidi made me happy there were no sharp objects in the vicinity. Fidi winced when they shook hands.

"This is Fidi," I said, searching desperately for a way to avoid having Christian out me in front of my colleagues. He'd never out me to be mean, but if I was hanging out with someone he'd assume was my boyfriend with my colleagues, it meant I was already out.

"We have this stupid game going on?" I said. That was *not* supposed to be a question.

I saw the moment Fidi understood. "Yeah, it's this stupid thing I do whenever I start in a new team. I see how close I can get before the guys freak out."

The look he was giving me was glacier cold.

Luckily, Christian only had eyes for me right now.

"Tristan here," Fidi continued, "apparently doesn't like to lose. I haven't managed to freak him out yet."

I swallowed hard as I held Christian's gaze. I hoped he could read the apology I couldn't give voice to.

"Yeah," Christian said, his voice so flat it was almost scary. "That's not quite what you need to freak this guy out."

Since we'd already thrown the last ball, most of our team were packing up, approaching the counter where they could retrieve their shoes. Sylvie and Laure were still hanging around, listening in on our little conversation.

I didn't like the speculative look in Sylvie's eyes.

Christian seemed to shake himself back to life. "I won't keep you guys any longer," he said. "Enjoy the rest of your weekend. Give my regards to your parents, will you, Tristan?"

I couldn't manage more than whisper. "Sure."

"Old friend, huh?" Fidi said once Christian was out of view.

Yeah, he knew.

I went to retrieve my stuff from under my seat, trying to get my heartbeat back to normal.

"He seemed nice," Sylvie said.

"Yeah, he's an old friend." I avoided eye contact.

"And cute."

This time I looked up, but Sylvie didn't meet my eyes. She was thumbing through her phone.

"If you say so." Comeback of the year.

TWENTY

Nobody's Dirty Little Secret

I CLOSED THE door to our room and leaned back against it.

Fidi walked to his side of the room and started removing his watch and placing it on the nightstand. "So, I'm guessing that Christian guy is an ex?"

"Yeah." I closed my eyes and took a deep breath. I couldn't remember ever feeling so exhausted. A long hike, an evening at the bowling alley laughing my ass off, then the stress of meeting Christian. I was going to sleep like the dead.

"Why did you break up?"

I opened my eyes and answered through clenched teeth. "Kind of a personal question, isn't it?" I sat down on the bed and removed my shoes.

"You don't have to answer."

I sighed. "It just became…too much. I felt pressured."

"To come out of the closet?"

Another sigh. I pulled my t-shirt off over my head, almost feeling like it required too much energy. "I guess. Stupidly enough, I was planning to come out for him, but he wouldn't let me do it under my conditions."

"What were your conditions?" I heard clothes rustling and then the bed dipped as Fidi got into bed.

I dropped my pants and socks on the floor and fell back on the soft mattress. I pulled the sheet up to my neck and reveled in the feeling of lying down, clean sheets, and having a warm body next to me.

"I don't really know," I said. "I just know that I was ready to come out, and I was looking for the right time and way to do it. I didn't like feeling like I was never good enough for him. I wondered if coming out at work would actually help. Or if our relationship was doomed anyway."

"So you ended it and removed the problem."

I flung an arm over my eyes, relishing the stretch in my back muscles. I probably should have stretched after our hike. "He was so insecure. I honestly don't think it would've lasted."

The mattress moved as Fidi turned onto his side to face me. I could feel his breath on my hand. "You know, if you just come out at work now, the issue will never be a problem with future boyfriends. They might still be insecure, but it will be easier to judge them by it if it's on a less important subject."

"You make it sound like coming out is the most important thing in the world."

"It is important," Fidi said. "To me, at least. Which is why I don't date closeted guys."

I lifted my arm to rest it above my head so I could meet Fidi's gaze. He was so close. I could just drown in the soft brown of his eyes. "Why is it so important to you? I don't see what other people should have to say about who I'm sharing my life with."

There was a spark of anger in his eyes as he answered. "I don't like being anybody's dirty little secret. If you want me, you own it."

"Fair enough." I allowed myself to study the softness of his hair and the smoothness of his skin. There was a good chance I wouldn't get this close again anytime soon. "I do own it, though. Outside of work. Christian met all my friends, and even my parents. It's just at work that I don't want people to think about my sex life when we're working."

Fidi lowered his head into his pillow so only half his face was visible. "It's called taking one for the team," he said. "It won't ever be considered normal if everybody stays in hiding."

"I know," I whispered. "And I will do it. One day. When I find the right guy."

"If you say so." Fidi closed his eyes and was asleep within seconds.

Even though my exhaustion was weighing down my eyelashes, I stayed awake for a long time just watching him sleep.

TWENTY-ONE

Glass Closet

JUST LIKE WE'D anticipated, it took the team the whole morning to clean the cabin and get ready to leave. The hangovers were much softer this time around, but sore muscles made our lives miserable. To everyone except Olivier, that is, who was in a terrific mood and didn't seem to feel yesterday's hike at all. Must be nice to be Superman.

After a quick lunch, we piled back into our cars and turned our noses homeward. Fidi fell asleep in less than ten minutes, and Laure and Denis once again spent the entire ride with their noses in their phones.

I was left with my own thoughts, playing the weekend over and over in my mind, reliving my nights with Fidi as often as our involuntary swim in the mountain lake. I'd had more fun than I'd had in ages.

When I pulled into our company's parking lot—eerily empty and quiet on a Sunday night—I exited my car to stretch my legs. I only had a twenty-minute drive to get to my apartment, but I was getting tired of driving. For the last half hour, I'd been having a wet dream about taking a hot shower to ease the aching muscles in my back.

Everybody said their goodbyes and drove off in their own cars.

As I got ready to get back into my own vehicle, I realized Fidi was still there, but there were no more cars in the parking lot. He squinted at his phone as he thumbed through some app.

"Don't you have your car?" I asked, my hand on the door handle.

Fidi looked up and blinked. "No," he answered. "I came by train. It's just less of a hassle."

I nodded. "And when's the next train?"

Fidi winced as he powered down his phone and shoved it in his back pocket. "In two hours."

"Get back in the car," I told him as I waved him over. "I'll drive you home."

Fidi crossed his arms over his chest. "I live in Albi," he reminded me. "That's an hour out of your way. Then another hour for you to get home."

I shrugged and opened the door. "It's no trouble. I didn't have anything planned for tonight anyway." There'd still be time for a hot shower when I got home.

He took a minute to think about it, but my offer must have been more attractive than waiting at the train station for two hours, so he eventually put his bag back in my trunk and buckled in next to me.

"You'll have to guide me," I told him. "I've never been to Albi."

Fidi shook his head. "How can you have lived in Toulouse for years and never visited Albi?"

"I grew up in Toulouse, that's how," I said. "It's a universal fact that you never visit anything too close to home."

"Fine." I could hear the smile in his voice. "First, you get out of this parking lot."

"Yes, sir," I replied and started the engine.

I was pretty sure he did it to annoy me, but I loved hearing his voice as he gave directions, so I never told him to stop, even when the signs indicating which direction to take for Albi were all over the place.

An hour later, I parked in front of a fairly new apartment building at the outskirts of Albi.

"Nice place," I said, suddenly awkward in the silence that settled when the engine died down.

Fidi leaned forward to look up at the building as if seeing it for the first time. He cocked his head to the side. "It's all right, I guess," he said. "It's just temporary until I buy my own place, but I keep changing projects and cities, so I never know where to settle down."

Silence again.

I didn't get out of the car because I just knew that would make for an even more awkward situation. But why wasn't Fidi getting out?

"Would you like to come up for a coffee or something?" he finally asked, his eyes still on the building in front of us.

"Uh." I was so surprised by his offer, my mind went blank and I had no idea how to answer him.

"Come on," Fidi said, his gaze finally meeting mine. "You've been driving for almost three hours now. It'll do you good to take a break before getting back on the road for yet another hour."

I nodded slowly. "Fair enough. I guess one cup of coffee won't hurt."

He rolled his eyes at me and opened his door. "Seriously, Tristan," he said as he got out. "Don't worry. Nobody from work is going to see you walking into the gay guy's apartment."

"I'm not worried." I got out of the car and helped Fidi with his bags in the trunk. "Have I still not proved that I'm not afraid to be seen with you?"

"I'm not sure what you've proved, honestly." He started walking toward the main entrance. "It's like you're in a glass closet or something. You're definitely in there, but don't care if anybody sees it."

"I don't even know what that means."

Fidi held the door for me, then ran a hand through his hair, making it stand up in the back. "Me, neither," he said. "I'm too tired for philosophical conversations right now."

"Coffee, then?"

"Coffee."

TWENTY-TWO

I Didn't Say Sex

Fidi's place was neat and cozy, though it was obvious that he wasn't planning on staying too long. It seemed like he'd put in the minimum effort required for it to feel like a real home, without doing anything too permanent or expensive.

The living room was spacious and filled with light, even in the late afternoon, and his couch was turned to face the large floor-to-ceiling windows instead of a TV, like most people did.

I looked around a second time. "No TV?"

"Everything on TV is crap," Fidi replied as he dumped his bags in front of what I assumed to be his bedroom door. "I watch the occasional film on my laptop, but there's just no point in me having an actual TV. Saves me a couple of hundred bucks a year on taxes, too." He shrugged.

"Fair enough." Hands in my back pockets, I rocked back on my heels, not quite knowing what to do with myself. I wasn't sure how welcome I really was in Fidi's space.

Fidi waved to the couch. "Sit down, Tristan. Relax. I'll make us some coffee." He huffed a sigh. "You look like you're afraid I'll jump you or something."

I barked a laugh as I settled in on his couch. "That's supposed to be your worry, not mine."

"What?" Fidi got two small cups out of his cupboards and set both on the shiny Nespresso machine on his kitchen counter. "I think I need the coffee before I'll be able to make sense of what you say. It takes real acrobatics of the mind to try to follow you."

I leaned my head back on the couch and closed my eyes. It had been a really great idea to take a break before getting back on the road—I was exhausted.

"Never mind," I said. Then, before my brain could catch up with my mouth. "You're the one not wanting to have sex again, is all. I'm game."

The sound of one of the cups clattering to the floor was followed by Fidi swearing—in multiple languages.

"Didn't even know you knew how to swear," I commented, eyes still closed. "You're always so clean and proper at work."

"That's because it's *work*, you idiot," Fidi said under his breath. "There's a time and a place for everything." It sounded like he put the cup on the counter and dried up the spilled coffee.

I'd have been incapable of opening my eyes if my life depended on it. I was in some sort of half-asleep state, where my body was completely immobile, but my mind was still somewhat working. My mouth seemed to have taken on a life of its own.

"Right now, right here, would be a really good place for sex," I said.

A cup breaking. More swearing.

"Come on!" Fidi's voice seemed panicked and out of breath. I could hear him taking heavy breaths as he cleaned up the second cup of coffee. A minute later, the couch dipped next to me as he sat down.

"Well," he said, his voice tense but closer to normal. "There will be no coffee."

"How about sex?" I finally managed to open my eyes and rolled my head on the side to look at Fidi.

He covered his face with his hands and made a sound that was somewhere between a growl and a scream. "What part of *no* do you not understand?"

I lifted my hand a couple of centimeters in a vague attempt to wave my hand. "I understand you just fine," I said. "I'm just trying to change it into a *yes*."

Fidi lowered his hands to his cheeks so he could meet my gaze. "By saying the word sex over and over?"

I gave him a flat look. "Is it not working?"

His hands went back over his eyes.

I was pretty sure it was working.

"I'm not asking to be boyfriends or anything," I argued. "I get that you don't want that. But are you also categorically against one-night stands? Two-night stands," I added after a moment's thought.

Fidi leaned forward to place his elbows on his knees and hung his head so his hair fell forward. "You're so fucked up."

"I'd like to fuck *you*."

"Oh my god!" Fidi threw his hands in the air as if actually asking God for help.

"Hey," I said, a smile stretching across my face though the rest of my body was still playing dead on the couch. "I didn't say sex."

"You just did!"

"Right." Silence fell and after a while my eyes closed again. I was in this wonderful place between asleep and awake, where I was aware of the fact that I was as good as sleeping. There's nothing better in the world than being aware of sleeping.

Except sex. I smiled to myself.

I was all the way asleep when Fidi's voice woke me. He was closer. Close enough for me to feel his breath on my cheek.

"You're too tired for sex anyway," he said.

I had a feeling he assumed I was dead to the world and I wasn't intended to actually hear him.

Without even opening my eyes, I lifted my hand to pull him to me. He tensed and drew in a quick breath as our lips met, but it didn't take long for him to melt against my side.

Fully aware that this was never going to happen again, I decided to make the most of it.

I used both hands to pull Fidi to my lap so he was sitting across my thighs. It made the kissing a little awkward because he towered above me, but the upside was that my hands were free to roam up his back, into his hair, down to his ass.

I groaned my appreciation.

Fidi seemed to be on the same page, if the mewling sounds he made were any indication.

I interrupted the kiss but held him close as we switched breath back and forth. "Is this okay?" I asked.

His dark eyes met mine, hardly any of the brown irises visible because of his dilated pupils. "One-night stand," he said between breaths. "Nothing more."

"Deal." And I delved back for another dose of his luscious lips.

TWENTY-THREE

I Have Other Plans

We continued kissing, but the position wasn't particularly comfortable for either of us. Also, I became increasingly aware of the floor-to-ceiling windows in front of us, giving any curious neighbor quite the view.

"Would you mind moving this to the bedroom?" I asked between kisses, while my hands explored Fidi's back, running up his spine and back down his sides.

Fidi arched into my touch and sighed. "Yeah," he said, breaking the kiss, leaving me feeling bereft. "Come with me."

We scrambled off the couch and Fidi dragged me after him down a short hallway and into his bedroom.

I hardly spared a glance at our surroundings, only noticing the fact that it had a large bed and curtained windows. That was all I really needed.

I wanted to throw Fidi down on his bed and have my way with him, but first things first. "Clothes off," I said as I started pulling his shirt over his head.

Fidi complied, helping me with the top buttons so the shirt wouldn't get stuck on his head, and opening his belt buckle. Then he seemed to realize he should change his priorities and started in on my clothes.

Ten seconds later, we were both naked and panting, back to kissing and enjoying the whole-body skin-to-skin contact.

My hands went to his ass, pulling him close to me so that our dicks could get reacquainted.

"Please tell me you have lube and condoms." I leaned in to get to that spot between his neck and his shoulder, enjoying the smell and taste that I was coming to identify as uniquely Fidi.

"Nightstand," Fidi replied, his voice rising to a squeak on the last syllable as I bit down gently on his neck.

"Thank God." I tore myself away from him for a second to reach for the nightstand and pull out the drawer. It was empty.

"The other one," Fidi said, pointing to an identical nightstand on the far side of the bed.

Growling, I pushed Fidi down on the bed below me and proceeded to crawl over him to reach for the far end of the bed. His hands skimmed my side as I moved up his body, and warm tingles followed his touch down the side of my torso, my hips, and my thighs.

I pulled open the drawer and fumbled around inside in search of the familiar packets while Fidi's hands went back up to my ass to give it a squeeze.

I found the condom, and then the lube. "You feel real good down th—"

I yelped as my dick was engulfed in warmth. I'd been dangling it in front of Fidi's face and he'd taken the opportunity to have a taste.

The condom and lube clutched in my hand, I looked down just in time to see Fidi swallowing me down to the root. His gorgeous lips stretched around me, and his tongue licked around my tip. Eyes open, he stared up at me to catch my reaction.

I didn't bother trying to hide how awesome he felt. My breath caught, my eyes drooped, and my mouth hung open in awe.

"So good," I rasped out. I had trouble finding words adequate for the situation. "Please don't stop." My hips started thrusting of their own accord. I tried stopping them for fear of overwhelming Fidi, but his grip on my ass tightened and encouraged me to keep going.

Fidi kept sucking me like I was his favorite flavor lollipop, and I kept fucking his mouth without ever blinking once, to make sure I didn't miss a single moment of the beauty of Fidi's mouth on my dick. After only a minute or two, I was close to coming.

"Stop," I said, pulling away from his mouth. "Or I'm going to come." I heaved a breath, trying to regain some composure. "Can't end this soon."

Fidi just grinned up at me and ran his hands up my chest to pinch my nipples. "It's not a problem if you come," he said. "That just means I'll be the one to fuck you."

My heart skipped a beat at that idea and I felt a blush crawl up my chest. I usually preferred topping, but it seemed like my body would be okay with bottoming for Fidi.

"Not today," I said with a growl. "Right now, I have other plans."

Surprise flickered across Fidi's face as I crawled down the bed so we would be face to face again. He must have heard the unspoken "maybe another time" in my statement. He hadn't expected me to ever bottom.

I was a little surprised by it myself, but didn't want to talk about it, so I went in for a kiss. Our tongues tangled like they'd had years of practice and I could taste myself on him. He was all soft lips, wet mouth, and hard body. Everything a guy could ask for.

I lost track of time as our hands and mouths explored each other's bodies. I learned that Fidi indeed had very little body hair, that he was ticklish on the inside of his thighs, and that he loved it when I sucked on his nipples. Fidi didn't take long to figure out that I loved it when his hands were on my ass, that I didn't like him getting close to my belly button, and that he could get away with anything while I was nuzzling into that spot on his neck.

Finally, I became too impatient to be inside him and came up for air so I could grab the lube where I'd dropped it on the bed.

Fidi opened to give me access and while I prepared him, our kisses grew so hot I couldn't tell which lips were his, which tongue was mine. My body was on fire, every nerve ending responding to Fidi's touch, and every muscle ready to give everything for his pleasure.

When neither of us could take any more waiting, Fidi rolled the condom on me before I settled between his thighs. He wrapped his legs around my back and his arms around my neck. Our eyes locked as I entered him.

I'd never seen anything more beautiful in my life.

"Beautiful," I whispered as I sheathed myself fully inside him. "So, so beautiful."

Fidi seemed beyond words. His eyes stayed on mine with a look of wonder and his hands roamed across my face, skimming across my cheekbones and through my stubble.

When I started moving, his eyes rolled back, and he arched his back on a blissful sigh.

I wouldn't turn down such an invitation. I latched onto his neck and let my instincts take over.

It didn't take long to find the angle that Fidi needed, and even less to find a rhythm that suited us both. As I moved in him, all I could feel was the smoothness of Fidi's skin, the firmness of his muscles, and the exquisite timbre of his sighs and moans. I felt like my body was no longer only mine, but ours, and couldn't tell the difference between his pleasure and mine.

It was all simply perfection.

When Fidi came, I followed right behind him, and we collapsed in a heap of exhausted limbs, breath heaving and muscles trembling.

"Thank you," I whispered when I'd caught my breath. "That was…" I couldn't find the right word.

"Yeah," Fidi agreed. "It was."

"Just a second, and I'll move," I promised. My entire weight was on him and that couldn't be comfortable.

"No worries," Fidi slurred.

We were both asleep within seconds.

TWENTY-FOUR

The Whole Wear-Inside-Out Thing

I AWOKE TO an unusual ring-tone, my head snapping up in surprise.

My first realization: I was drooling. My second: I was drooling on Fidi's smooth chest.

Third: It was morning.

Fidi was waking up beneath me, hair mussed and standing up in all directions, and eyes bleary.

"What time is it?" I asked, my voice gravelly.

"Uh…" Fidi blinked several times and tried to draw a deep breath.

I moved off his chest to allow the poor guy some air.

"It's probably seven thirty," he said. He crawled halfway out of bed to reach his pants and stop the alarm that was still ringing on his phone. Blinking again to focus on the screen, he cleared his throat. "Yeah. Seven thirty-one."

"*Merde.*" I hastily wiped my chin with the back of my hand and looked around for my clothes. My shirt was by the door, my pants at the foot of the bed, and my boxers on the top of a dresser in the corner. We'd clearly been in a rush to get that one off.

Out of the corner of my eye, I saw Fidi stare at the bed. I glanced back, wondering what had him so mesmerized.

The used condom lay in the very middle of the bed, crumpled and still carrying its load.

I couldn't even remember pulling out the night before, and definitely not tying off the condom. Had I slept with the thing on my dick all night? Gross.

"Sorry, I'll get rid of that," I said and quickly scooped it up. Then I just stood there, naked and with a used condom in my hand.

"There's a trash can in the bathroom," Fidi said, clearly understanding my dilemma. He wrinkled his nose as he gingerly touched his abdomen.

Right. I looked down and realized I was in much the same state. We were both covered in Fidi's dried cum.

This was not shaping up to be a good day.

"Why don't you take a shower while you're in there," Fidi said with a wave in direction of his bathroom. "I'll get the coffee started."

Normally, I'd have argued for him to go first, or offered for him to join me. But I had to be at work in an hour, and I was too far away for that to be even marginally feasible.

"Thank you," I said, making sure I made eye contact so he understood how much I appreciated it.

"Don't mention it." He eyed our clothes strewn around on the floor. "Do you need any clean clothes?"

I shook my head. "I just need to get out of here as soon as possible so I can go home and change."

Fidi checked the time on his phone. "There's no way you'll have time to take a shower, drive through traffic to your place and change, then get back into traffic, and still be on time for our nine o'clock meeting. Why don't you borrow some clothes from me and just go straight to the office?"

As the panic took hold, I felt my heart race and cold sweat appear on my forehead. I had a meeting with Dimitri every Monday morning to give him an update on how we were doing on our security breach. Fidi was right. There was no way I could do the tour of the city and still be on time for the meeting.

I racked my brain, trying to remember what clothes I'd packed for the weekend. "I can wear the same pants," I said. "And I think I have a clean shirt in my car. But I'm out of clean underwear." I looked at the pair on the dresser. "Maybe I can test the whole wear-inside-out thing."

"Yuck." Fidi shrugged. "I'll find you a pair of boxers. And I'll get your stuff in from the car."

I wasn't exactly in the habit of borrowing other guys' underwear, but it did sound more appealing than wearing yesterday's boxers. "Thank you."

Fidi nodded. "Now get moving. We have to be out the door by eight, or there's no guarantee we'll be in the office by nine. I need at least fifteen minutes in there."

"Don't worry," I replied, already moving toward the bathroom door. "I only need ten."

TWENTY-FIVE

Purple Underwear is Clearly the Ultimate Proof of Homosexuality

WE MADE IT on time for the meeting. Nobody saw us carpooling in the morning, and nobody seemed to notice anything amiss.

I couldn't believe such a catastrophic morning could possibly even out that soon.

Even the car ride had been nice, with both of us avoiding the topic of last night's romp in the sack as if it had never happened, and just moved straight to talking about work and our assessment of our new colleagues.

A little past three in the afternoon, I was helping Sylvie figure out how to get out of a coding dilemma. At first, I stood next to her seat, sometimes standing straight, sometimes leaning on her desk when I needed to see her lines of code. After a while, I got tired of standing, and squatted down on my haunches to at least use a different set of muscles.

Sylvie continued her explanation of why her code seemed to go into an infinite loop whenever the user launched Media Player at the same time as our application. It was one of those situations where you just stared accusingly at the sky, wondering *why?*

"Dude," Olivier said from his seat behind me. "You're taking this game with Fidi too far. He's going to end up turning you at this rate."

My breath caught, but luckily Olivier wouldn't be able to see my expression from where he was seated.

What was he talking about? Had he seen us arrive together that morning and come to the right conclusion? Or at least close enough to hurt?

A stray thought popped into my head. *So what if they knew?*

I'd always said I'd come out at work once I met a guy who might make it worth the hassle. Could Fidi be that guy? Would he go out with me—for more than just a one-night stand—if I told the team about my sexual preferences? That did seem to be the case, since Fidi certainly hadn't minded our activities last night. His only objections had turned around my being in the closet.

What if I turned to face Olivier and said, "Actually, he didn't need to turn me, I was already batting for his team?"

Would that really be so bad?

Sylvie spoke before I could work up the nerve to actually talk. "What are you going on about now, Olivier?"

"His boxers," Olivier said. "They're the type that Fidi always wears. With flashy, girly colors."

I closed my eyes in resignation. When I'd crouched down, my shirt had ridden up, and my pants down, showing the elastic of the boxers Fidi had lent me this morning. True to form, he'd only given me the choice between pink and purple.

"Purple isn't a girly color," I said as I straightened and pulled my shirt back down.

"Yes, it is." Olivier wore a shit-eating grin as he leaned back in his chair with his hands folded behind his head, enjoying his fun.

Sylvie swung her chair around to face Olivier. "Are you saying that wearing purple underwear makes a guy gay?"

"Uh huh."

"That's ridiculous." Sylvie crossed her arms across her chest, apparently ready to do battle on my behalf on the subject of the color of my underwear.

I was starting to recognize the off-kilter feeling from that morning. The world might not be done with me yet.

Of course, Fidi chose that moment to enter the room. "What's going on?" he asked when he saw Olivier and Sylvie squaring off.

"Tristan is wearing purple underwear," Olivier said, his eyes gleaming as he studied Fidi's reaction to this news.

"Oh." Fidi's eyes went from Olivier's grin, to Sylvie's frown, to my—most likely—panicked look. "And that's important why?"

"Olivier, here," Sylvie said, voice dripping with venom, "thinks this means that you've *turned* him to your side. Purple underwear is clearly the ultimate proof of homosexuality."

I wondered if my face was red from blushing or white from shock. The waves of hot and cold that kept running through me could mean either.

Just a minute ago, I'd thought about telling the team I was gay, and now that the subject had come up, I was in complete panic mode at the thought. Guess what looks good in practice isn't always so easy to go through with in reality.

Fidi once again scanned the room. "Well," he said. He put his hands on his hips, then crossed them over his chest. "I don't know if I have anything useful to say on that subject. I certainly have purple underwear."—Did he ever, I was wearing one of them.—"But I am gay, so… A implies B is not equivalent to B implies A."

Olivier frowned at him. "You're no fun," he said, his arms falling down to his lap. "I thought you'd jump on an opportunity like this."

Fidi huffed. "I fight my own battles, thank you very much. I don't need your help." He met my gaze. "Dimitri wants to see us ASAP."

"Really?" Dread filled my stomach. "But we just met with him this morning."

Fidi met my eyes and I saw my own worry reflected there. "I know."

Dimitri's office was just down the hall, so we didn't have time to talk, except for Fidi to tell me he didn't know what was going on, either.

"Tristan, Fidi," Dimitri said as we entered his office. "Please close the door behind you."

I did as instructed, then forced myself to sit down in one of the visitors' chairs next to Fidi, and folded my hands in my lap.

Dimitri was efficient, as usual. "The client knows of the leaked data," he said.

Well, fuck.

"How much does he know?" I asked.

"You'll find out tomorrow," Dimitri replied. "I've been told they've learned that their data is for sale on the black market."

"So they might not know the leak was our fault?" Fidi asked.

Dimitri shook his head. "The time for hiding and subterfuge is passed. From now on, we share everything with the client and work with him to find and punish the culprit." He nodded to

Fidi. "I want you to officially make inquiries about the data at once and rediscover the fact that the data was surely leaked by our team. Everything you find—or have found up until now—will be shared in the meeting tomorrow. We play full transparency."

I pursed my lips. "Except for the fact that we've known about it for a month."

Dimitri's narrowed eyes met mine. "Obviously. You told me this morning that you were close to identifying the person trying to sell the data?"

Fidi nodded.

"Make sure you get better than just 'close.' We need to contain the data and catch the thief before the situation gets out of hand."

"Will do," Fidi said.

"I'll tell the team," I said. "I assume it's finally time to put them in the loop?"

Dimitri nodded and rapped his knuckles on the table. The meeting was adjourned.

Back out in the hallway with Dimitri's door closed behind us, Fidi murmured so nobody would overhear in the neighboring offices. "Want me to come with for the announcement? Two pairs of eyes to analyze people's reactions should be better than one."

"Thank you," I said. "Guess it's a good thing we got a good night's sleep yesterday. I have a feeling the next one's not going to be so relaxing."

"No kidding." Fidi ran his hands over his face several times. "I think I just might end up sleeping here if I can't get a breakthrough on that damned thief."

I straightened my back and went to meet my team. The war we'd been preparing for had just begun.

☙

WITHOUT SURPRISE, NOBODY confessed to being the data thief during my briefing. Nor did anyone look particularly guilty. The only thing that varied from one person to the other was the level of surprise or awareness of what this would mean for our team and the company.

Laure seemed to have been unaware that the data could have value. Denis seemed to feel guilty that it had happened while he was Tech Lead for the team. Sylvie and most of the rest of the team appeared to understand the gravity of the situation but didn't feel any particular need to take responsibility for it.

Olivier asked lots of questions about when the theft had happened, probably to know if it had happened on his watch or on mine. I had to admit to judging him a little for not realizing this was *the reason* I'd come to replace him.

Not wanting the team to know we'd kept this from them for over a month, I bit the bullet and said we didn't know when the theft had happened, but that we'd learned about it today.

In any case, that meeting was peanuts compared to the meeting I had with the client the next day.

TWENTY-SIX

Those People

Dimitri, Fidi, and myself all showed up in our best suits for the client meeting the next day. I'd forgone the tie because it made me so uncomfortable I was afraid it would impede on my capacity to perform during the meeting, but the suit was the one I wore to marriages and the shirt was ironed to a crisp.

Fidi looked fabulous in a clear grey suit, pink shirt, and purple tie, though he kept drawing his fingers through his hair in what was clearly a nervous gesture and as a result, his hair was messier than usual.

It made me think of when I'd been the one to mess up his hair, which didn't really help with my concentration. But it did help on my nerves.

The grandfatherly image Monsieur Houliez usually projected during our weekly meetings was nowhere to be seen today. In his place, we were met by an unsmiling statue with a serious frown and dangerously angry eyes.

"You come in force, I see," he said when Dimitri entered the meeting room behind Fidi. "Good. At least you are taking the situation seriously."

"We most certainly are," I assured him as I took my seat and opened my laptop. "We've been working on retrieving the data and identifying the culprit from the very moment we found out about the breach."

I hoped he wouldn't ask when exactly that was.

Fidi sat down on my left and Dimitri next to him. The plan was for me to take the lead during the meeting. Dimitri was there to show he was present and to prove we were taking it seriously, but he left the dirty work to us.

"And what have you found?" Monsieur Houliez's fingers drummed a staccato beat on the table. He sat sideways on his chair, as if ready to get up and leave if he wasn't happy with what we said. Or possibly to let fists fly. Seeing his current mood, it didn't seem impossible.

Fidi drew out a sheet of paper from his notebook. This was his cue.

"We've managed to track down the database that has been put up for sale," Fidi said. "And see a partial extract."

He glanced up to gauge Monsieur Houliez's reaction on the next part. "As some manually modified test data were present, it's fairly obvious that the leak came from someone in our company." He swallowed. "This particular data set would not be available anywhere else."

Monsieur Houliez had kept his gaze on Fidi's notes during Fidi's delivery. Now he stared me down. "And what are you doing to stop the data from being sold to our competition?"

"We're in contact with the seller—" Fidi started.

"Have you identified the thief?" Monsieur Houliez seemed only to have eyes for me, even though Fidi was answering his questions.

"Once we have the data—"

The client cut Fidi short again. "What guarantee do I have that this is the only leak you've caused? How can I know it won't happen again?"

With a pinch in my heart for Fidi, I started answering as best I could. If the client only wanted to talk to me, he'd get me. And it would be too bad for him if I got something wrong.

"We're in contact with the seller," I said, meeting the man's angry eyes and forcing my own to project controlled calmness. "It shouldn't be long until we're able to draw him or her out enough to get our hands on the data and get it off the market. That is, at the moment, our first priority."

Fidi slid his notes in front of me and I shot him a grateful look. "As a close second, like you just said, we're looking to find the culprit in our team. If someone consciously took the data and tried to sell it, I'm confident we'll find him or her in the end. But if it was done out of ignorance of best practices, we might never know who did it."

Monsieur Houliez's fingers were still drumming on the table. His face was flushed, and his dark eyes bore into me. "Is your team really that unaware of the required security measures to apply when handling sensitive data?"

I gritted my teeth in the face of his onslaught. It hurt all the more for him being right. "All our employees have followed an awareness on security, I assure you, Monsieur Houliez. They *should* know what the risks are. But, as of right now, I've not had the time to talk to my team one-on-one to see if some of them took the rules too lightly. This *will* be done, but it was not our number one priority yesterday or this morning."

Monsieur Houliez seemed somewhat mollified by my answers. The drumming didn't stop, but it slowed—a little.

"We've instated several security measures over the past months," Fidi said. His voice was weaker than usual, an insecure note that I'd never heard before creeping into his speech.

Fidi might as well not have spoken.

"I'll expect a detailed report every night until this is over," Monsieur Houliez said. "On what you've found, and on what you've done to make sure it never happens again."

I swallowed. "Certainly."

"If I may," Dimitri said into the silence that followed. "We will do everything in our power to defend ourselves and your company and application against external attacks of any kind. But I trust you know that there is no such thing as zero risk. We can make sure that your average Sunday hacker can't get to your data, but if the real professionals really want to get in, they will."

Monsieur Houliez's hand flattened on the table, plunging the meeting room into silence. "I am aware. More than your team, clearly."

With that, the meeting was adjourned.

Dimitri and Fidi filed out, but as I got up, Monsieur Houliez held me back with a hand on my elbow. "Monsieur Marty," he said. "We've not worked together for long, but you seem to be fairly decent at your job."

"Thank you." I eyed him warily, wondering where he was going.

"Your colleague, however, I have less faith in."

I blinked. "Who, Fidisoa?"

"Yes, the man with the endless unpronounceable name. Are you quite certain he's taking this situation seriously enough?"

"Well, of course he is." I was searching my brain for any reason why the client might think Fidi was anything but professional but came up with a blank. "He basically worked through the night last night, to do his best to protect your data. He's one of our best experts on security issues."

Monsieur Houliez seemed to chew on that as he studied me.

"I don't like it," he finally said. "Those people can never take work seriously enough. They spend too much time partying, or putting on lotion, or whatever."

My breath seemed stuck in my chest. I could neither get it in nor out. "Those people?" It was close to a squeak.

"You know what I mean," Monsieur Houliez said, his voice firm. "I have nothing against them in general. But I don't trust him to manage this crisis properly."

Mind reeling, I just stood there with my mouth partly open.

I'd never actually been face to face with someone homophobic before. I knew they existed, had seen them on TV, heard them on the radio. But never to my face. Never for real

I was frozen to the spot.

Monsieur Houliez didn't seem to realize he'd just knocked my world off its axis. "I trust you'll take care of it," he said before leaving the meeting room.

I was left alone in an empty meeting room, with shaking breath and a broken heart.

TWENTY-SEVEN

A Coward and a Fake

Fidi and Dimitri were waiting for me in the parking lot next to the badge office. Dimitri's focus was on Fidi while he talked, and Fidi's eyes were on the ground.

I wasn't ready to face them. For once, I prayed for a long line at the badge office to retrieve my ID papers, but no such luck.

When I walked up to the pair, Dimitri was still talking.

"—will have no impact on your career whatsoever." Dimitri glanced up at me as I approached. "Unfortunately, this just happens from time to time. The client needs a scapegoat and we have no say in who they pick. Didn't you have something similar on that project for Henley Motors some years back, Tristan?"

"Yes." My voice came out in a croak and I cleared my throat. "We had a two-month delay on a delivery and the client decided it was all the Tech Lead's fault for choosing the wrong architecture."

Dimitri nodded. "If I remember correctly, the Tech Lead *could* have anticipated the problems from the start, but only if he'd been psychic and known exactly the kind of changes of heart the client would have come up with months before if happened.

"We all know there is no way this situation is your fault." Dimitri put a hand on Fidi's shoulder and squeezed. "The problem occurred before you ever entered the project and I'm well aware of everything you've done to save the project since you came on. If anything, this experience will boost your career within our company."

Of course, if Fidi had ever had any ambition of getting hired by the client someday, that ship had officially sailed.

Fidi's eyes were still on the ground. His breathing was shallow, and he kept swallowing.

I couldn't decide if he was angry or sad—and I didn't know which option I preferred.

My own heart pounded along at top speed in my chest and my brain was stuck in a loop of *he accused Fidi because he's gay*. Monsieur Houliez had needed a scapegoat and decided that Fidi was his guy because, clearly, gay guys could never be trusted with anything important.

And I'd just stood there, silent.

I should have stood up for Fidi. Explained that if it weren't for him, we'd be in even more trouble. That he was the one person on the team who knew more about security than the rest of the group combined.

I should have told him that Fidi being gay had no impact whatsoever on his work.

I should have told him that I'm gay, too.

A frisson went through my body at the thought and I had to catch myself from shaking like a leaf in front of my boss.

That last thought scared me a lot more than it should have. I'd claimed for years that I wouldn't mind coming out at work once I met the right guy. I wasn't ashamed of who I was, I just enjoyed my privacy. And yet the idea of Monsieur Houliez or Dimitri finding out about me made me want to run and hide.

I'm a coward and a fake.

When neither Fidi nor I had anything to say, Dimitri herded us toward the parking lot. "I'm not going back to the office straight away," he said. "I have another meeting across town. Tristan, would you mind taking Fidi back with you?"

"Sure." My voice was still not back to normal, dammit.

I shook hands with Dimitri and agreed to meet in his office that afternoon for a detailed run-through of the disastrous meeting and validation of the battle plan.

Fidi slid into the passenger seat of my car, buckled up, and held the bag with his laptop to his chest as if it were a shield.

He still hadn't met my eyes.

"I, uh…I'm really sorry," I said as I pulled out of the parking lot. The car was hot like a furnace from standing in the sun for the past hour and I cranked the air conditioning up to its max, grateful for once for the noise it made.

"It's not your fault," Fidi said, his voice flat.

I heaved an unsteady sigh. "Still. That wasn't cool of him."

Fidi picked at the seam of his bag. "Guess he had to choose someone."

"No, he didn't." I gripped the steering wheel so hard my knuckles whitened. "When we do a good job it's a team effort. I don't see why it should be any different when we fail. It's not possible for *one* person to be responsible for this kind of a mess."

Fidi huffed. "Technically, it *is* one person's fault. We just haven't figured out who yet." He leaned his head back on the headrest and gazed out the window. "Guess that'll be my motivation for nailing the guy."

I kept my eyes on the road and squeezed the steering wheel so hard it gave off a squeaking noise.

In my peripheral vision, I saw Fidi turning to look at me for the first time since the meeting.

"That should do it, right, Tristan?" he said, his voice oddly neutral. "We catch the bad guy and tell the client, and I'm off the hook. Right?"

I swallowed. "That should do it."

"Mhm." He kept silent for several seconds as he studied me. "What did he have to say to you once you were alone with him in the end there?"

My heart rate spiked and a drop of sweat rolled down my cheek. The air conditioning really should be having more of an effect by now.

"Nothing much," I said. "Just repeating how important this was and putting on some extra pressure for us to fix it immediately."

Fidi fell silent, but I could feel his gaze on me as I drove. I usually liked it when I had his attention, but now it made me want to jump out of my skin. Preferably also out of the car.

As I turned into our company's parking lot, he spoke up again. "Finding the culprit isn't going to help, is it?"

I pulled into a spot, turned off the ignition, and pulled the brake. I searched for an answer in the bushes in front of my car but came up empty.

Fidi didn't seem to need and answer. "Just tell me one thing, Tristan. Is it the foreigner thing, or the gay thing?"

I couldn't bring myself to look at him. "I don't…" I couldn't tell him the truth and I couldn't lie.

"I see," Fidi said, disappointment clear in those two short words. "You said nothing, didn't you?"

I looked down in my lap. Opened my mouth to answer. Nothing came out.

"Did you agree with him? To suck it up a little extra to the client?" The flatness in Fidi's voice was giving way to anger.

I finally found my voice. "No! Of course not."

Fidi sighed. "Well," he said, "I guess you can sleep well tonight then." He opened the car door.

"Fidi—" I pleaded.

He jumped out and slammed the door in my face.

TWENTY-EIGHT

I Was Desperate

I HADN'T EXPECTED to see Fidi again for the rest of the day—or for the rest of my life, for that matter. He'd secluded himself in one of the tiny four-person meeting rooms since we got back, apparently working on tracking down our lost data.

My concentration had been shot to hell by that morning's meeting, so I had my suspicions Fidi would be in much the same state, but I had no intention of calling him on it.

I busied myself with finalizing the Security Assurance Plan and sending it to Monsieur Houliez as proof of how seriously we took the project's security.

At half past four in the afternoon, Fidi appeared in the door to our office. "Tristan, you have a minute?" He spoke in my general direction but didn't meet my eyes.

"Sure," I said, locked my laptop, and followed him down the hall to the room he'd used as an office.

He closed the door behind me and leaned against it. "I have the name of the guy selling our data," he said.

I jerked as I was sitting down, almost missing the chair in the process. "You did? Who is it?"

Fidi shrugged. "Some guy named Cédric Massotier. A computer engineer working for some small start-up across town. Have you heard of him?"

I shook my head. "Name doesn't ring a bell."

Fidi sat down in front of his laptop and logged in. "As far as I can tell, the company he works for is not a competitor or anything. I can't see any motive in wanting to torpedo us. Looks like he just wants the money he can get for the data."

"How did you find him?"

Fidi rolled his eyes as he scanned through something on his laptop. "I pretended to want to buy the data and said I wanted to come pick it up in person to get it on an untraceable memory stick." He met my eyes briefly. "I was desperate."

I cocked my head. "And he fell for that?"

"Yeah." Fidi huffed a laugh. "I'd find it funny except it's our data he's managed to get his hands on and he's brought us a world of pain for his troubles."

I rolled the extensible line on my badge around my finger and let it slap back in place. It was a good back-up occupation for my fingers when I forgot to bring a pen to a meeting. "Have you given this information to the police yet? I suppose that's the next step?"

Fidi shook his head and met my gaze for a fraction of a second. "Not yet," he said. "I wanted to tell you first."

"Thank you." I wanted to tell him how sorry I was about that morning, but I had no idea how to say it.

Fidi made a couple of clicks with his mouse, then closed his laptop. "I'll go to the police right now. They can come with me to the rendezvous. Should I tell Dimitri, or do you want the honors?"

I mustered a smile, though Fidi wouldn't see it since he was avoiding looking at me like I was the sun. "I'll let you do it. You did the work, after all. Tell him I assume he'll want to be the one to tell the client, will you?" I ran a hand through my hair and sighed. "I don't suppose you found a link to any of our team members during your research?"

"No, I didn't. Feel free to look for it. I'm about ninety percent certain that the leak was accidental, so we might never find out who did it." He grabbed his computer and opened the door.

"You're probably right," I said. "Thank you, Fidi. We couldn't have done all this without you."

Finally, he met my eyes, but it was a hollow victory. The hurt and anger I saw in his beautiful brown eyes cut me to the bone and left me without breath. I'd helped put that pain there. I'd stood by and let him get hurt.

"I know," he said. He studied me for a moment as if searching for something.

He must not have found what he was looking for because he gave a tiny shake of his head, then headed down the hallway toward Dimitri's office.

I lowered my head into my hands and gave myself just one minute to wallow in my misery before I went to talk to my team.

TWENTY-NINE

That's My Cousin

"All right, everyone," I said as I entered the office. "Can I have your attention for just a minute, please?"

I'd pulled the guys from the second office with me, so I had everyone except Fidi in one room. They arrayed across the space, the people who belonged in this office on their chairs, the others leaning against desks or the window sill.

"I have one short announcement to make," I said, "but first, I just wanted to check something." I wasn't big on lying and subterfuge, but I wanted to try just one thing before asking the team straight out about the leaked data.

"I just received a new resume." I tapped on my phone, pretending to read something. "A guy named Cédric Massotier.

Seems to have an interesting profile, but since he's local, I just wanted to see if any of you knew him."

I kept my expression neutral and pretended to be just vaguely interested in their reactions, but I was alert for the smallest movement.

Mathieu cocked his head as he mouthed the name but didn't seem to come up with anything.

Laure tapped something in on her phone and studied the results—she either couldn't care less or was Googling the guy. In either case, she didn't seem to have any prior knowledge of him.

Olivier frowned at me. It took me a moment to realize he wasn't reacting to the name of the guy, but to the fact that I was looking at resumes. We were already somewhat overstaffed with two Project Managers and two Tech Leads. Why would I want to hire yet another guy?

"Hey, that's my cousin!" Sylvie's face lit up with a smile as she leaned forward in her chair. "I didn't know he was looking to change jobs. If I'd known, I'd have passed on his resume myself."

For a minute, I didn't know how to react. My little charade had worked.

Now what?

I glanced around the room, at the expectant faces of my team members. What would happen if I told them Sylvie was most likely the source of all our recent troubles? Would they turn on her? Would it ruin team morale?

Was there really any point in anyone finding out?

Mathieu cleared his throat. "What was the announcement?"

"Huh?" My mind was suddenly blank.

"You said you had an announcement to make?" Wiry arms crossed, Mathieu shrugged. "I'm guessing you don't need all of us to listen in when Sylvie tells you about her cousin. So what was that other thing?"

"Oh. Right." I tried rearranging my thoughts as my heart thumped in my chest. I'd never been a big fan of confrontations, but this reaction wasn't normal, even for me. It would seem like the awfulness of Monsieur Houliez's accusations yesterday had left more of an impression than I'd have liked.

"Fidi figured out who stole our data," I said, my voice flat.

"That's great!"

"Who is it?"

"Has he called the cops?"

They were all thrilled, including Sylvie who pumped a victorious hand in the air, and their euphoria lifted a weight off my chest and allowed me to think clearly again.

"Fidi is calling the cops as we speak and will most likely assist them in catching our culprit shortly."

"So who is it?" Mathieu uncrossed his arms and put his hands on his hips instead, looking like he was ready to run after the bad guy as soon as he had a name.

I waved a dismissive hand. "Just some guy. I'd never heard of him before."

Frowning, Mathieu shifted his weight from one foot to the other. "You're not going to tell us?"

Letting out a short breath, I shook my head. "No. I don't think there's any point, really. We're handling it. We don't need you running after the guy. We need you to do your best to repair our reputation with the client."

Laure was rearranging her barrette in her hair again, making sure today's lily sat right above her left ear. "So, basically, go back to work?"

I offered her a genuine smile. "Basically, yes." I turned to Sylvie. "Would you mind coming with me so we can have a quick talk about your cousin?"

"Sure." She sprang out of her chair to follow me. "My pleasure."

I led her to the tiny meeting room Fidi had recently vacated and closed the door behind her.

Sylvie smiled at me. "I really didn't know Cédric was looking for work. I thought he was happy where he was."

I nodded. I could have asked her a couple of more questions before breaking the news, but I just hated the duplicity of it all. "I haven't actually received his resume," I said. "He's the one who stole our data."

"What?" Her smile fell off her face in an instant. The stricken look taking its place confirmed that she hadn't knowingly been part of the theft.

Still, I needed to know if she'd had an unknowing part, because I had to be absolutely sure that we'd closed the door the thief had come through. If it hadn't been through Sylvie, it meant we had a different weakness somewhere that could be exploited again.

I met Sylvie's eyes to let her read the truth there. "Fidi managed to set up a meeting with him today, to buy the database. He gave his name and address. We'll only know for sure once we get our hands on the actual database, but I find it highly unlikely that he's innocent."

Shoulders slumped, Sylvie folded her hands on the table in front of her and studied her nails. "Why did you need to talk to me, then? To ask if I thought he'd done it?" She heaved a breath and gulped. "I'd really like to think he didn't."

"But you don't think it's impossible?"

She sighed again. "I don't know. If what you say is true, the evidence does sound damning. But no, I've never known him to do anything nefarious. Not that we hang out all that often."

"When was the last time you saw him?"

She pulled a hand through her blonde hair as she thought. "Two or three months maybe? I had several cousins over for dinner some time ago. I don't think I've seen him since."

The dates sounded about right. I softened my voice but kept eye contact. "Did you have your laptop with you at home that night?"

Sylvie's brows drew into a frown. "Probably. I usually take it home with me, like they tell us to do."

I nodded. "And do you think you happened to have a copy of our testing database on there? Could Cédric have had access to it at some point during the evening?"

As she realized the implications of my questions, Sylvie's eyes widened. "You think that's how he got his hands on it?" Her voice cracked on the last words.

I took a chance and covered her hands with one of mine. "At this point, Sylvie, that's what I'm hoping. It's not cool if that's how he got the database, but that would mean we've found the source of the theft, and don't have some back door standing wide open for anyone to step through."

Staring at our hands, Sylvie nodded. "I guess that makes sense." She closed her eyes and took a couple of deep breaths. "My laptop might have been turned on and unlocked that evening," she said in a small voice. "My own computer was acting up for a while—might have been around then—so I sometimes used the work laptop for music. Which means everyone probably touched the laptop at one point or another to pick a song."

The hurt in her eyes made me think of Fidi just minutes earlier when he'd left me to take care of the data thief. "Why would he violate my trust and jeopardize my work like that?"

I squeezed her hand. "I don't know, Sylvie. You know him better than I do. But my guess would be he thought it would be easy money. That's usually the main reason behind these things."

Sylvie retrieved her hand from under mine and covered her face. "What does this mean for me?"

"I can't give you any guarantees right away," I said. "I'll need to discuss it with Dimitri. But I'll push for not letting the team know he was your cousin or that he got the data from your laptop. There's really no need. This will probably be on your file here at the company, but I'm guessing you won't have much of a clap-back. What you did was neglect, not purposeful, and it can happen to anybody. And I'm assuming it will never happen again."

"You can bet your ass it won't," Sylvie hissed through clenched teeth.

"Great." I slapped a hand on the table and stood from my chair. "I'll let you get back to work. Just one thing." I held out a hand to stop her from opening the door just yet. "Don't contact your cousin, or talk about this with any friends of family, until the whole thing has played out, okay?"

Sylvie nodded, her eyes on the door. "Of course." After a moment's hesitation, she met my eyes. "Will you thank Fidi for me? Tell him I in no way blame him for this? He was just doing his job—and well, at that."

I released Sylvie and opened the door for her. "I'll tell him."

If he ever let me talk to him again.

THIRTY

I Almost

Claire called me while I was on my way home from work. She wanted to hang out, but I just didn't feel like having any company. I thought I'd made a pretty good job of convincing her I was just tired, but clearly it was an epic fail, because when I reached my apartment, she was waiting for me by the front door.

"I said I wasn't in the mood to hang out," I said to her as I unlocked the door, never meeting her eyes.

"No," she replied in a light tone. "You said a bunch of nonsensical mono-syllable words, most of which had nothing to do with my questions."

My eyes shot up to hers as I pushed the door open. Had I really been that out of it?

"Kidding," she said, walking through the door, kicking off her shoes, and marching in to sprawl on my couch. "But the fact that you can't even remember what you said to me proves that I was right to come here." She stared into my eyes. "You need to spill."

Sighing, I dropped my bag by the door and placed my shoes on the shoe rack before shuffling into the living room. "There's nothing to spill."

"Yes, there is."

"Fine. There is." I sat down on one of my rickety wooden dining room chairs but shot right back up. "Do you want anything to drink?"

"Sure." At my unvoiced questions, Claire answered, "Anything. Preferably with alcohol."

"Beer it is, then." While I was in the kitchen, I took a couple of deep breaths to prepare myself. I knew I needed to talk to someone, and my best friend really was the ideal option. But I didn't want to. I just wanted to forget that today ever happened.

Maybe it was time to turn today's theme of me being a coward around. I could, just to make myself feel a tiny little bit better about myself, work up the courage to tell my friend about my day. Who knows, maybe it could give me the balls to at least stand up for my coworker and friend at work tomorrow, even if I wouldn't stand up for myself.

I handed Claire her beer and slumped into the couch next to her. She promptly put her feet in my lap.

"All right. Spill." Sending me an annoyed glare when she discovered I hadn't opened her beer, she grabbed mine and used it to open hers. Which left me with an unopened bottle of beer in my hand and no energy to get up to open it.

I curled my hand around the bottle, enjoying its coolness on my skin as I leaned my head back on the backrest and closed my eyes.

"The client found out we'd waylaid some of his data yesterday," I started, talking to the ceiling.

Claire said nothing but nudged her foot into my thigh to tell me to keep going.

I gulped. "We already knew about it and had been trying to find the thief for a while. Well, Fidi had been tracking him."

"That's the cute guy you were crushing on."

"Yes." I paused for a moment, as a bad taste filled my mouth. Calling Fidi my crush felt inadequate after everything we'd been through over the last couple of weeks.

Claire growled and gave me another push in the legs. "You're back to mono-syllables, Tristan."

"Sorry." I sighed. I'd really have loved a sip of my beer, but there was no way I was getting off this couch anytime soon. "The client was pissed, obviously, and needed a scapegoat. He picked Fidi."

"*Was* he the culprit?"

"No. Couldn't have been. He wasn't brought onto the project until we knew about the theft. Just like me. We were brought in to fix everything."

I heard her gurgle down some of her beer. "You didn't tell me that before."

"Wasn't important," I said. "Who cares."

"Well, you care about *something* in this mess. Are you afraid this Fidi guy will take the fall for something he didn't do?"

I brought my bottle up to my forehead, seeking to soak up its coolness. "I know he's going to take the fall. The client's not going to change his tune even when he learns the truth."

"What makes you say that?"

"Because," I spat out, the venom in my voice making it crack, "as the client said, Fidi is one of *those guys*, who never take anything seriously, who can't be trusted with anything important." I squeezed my bottle of beer, wishing it was something that would break under pressure. "Just add a little bit of stress, and the truth comes spilling forth."

I received an armful of Claire as she threw herself in my lap. She took my head in both hands and shook it until I opened my eyes and looked at her. Her brown eyes were angry, but in a mother-hen kind of way.

"When did this happen?" she asked.

"Today," I answered.

She shook my head, scraping her long nails along my scalp. "You're lucky it wasn't any longer, or I would have killed you for not coming to talk to me. But you weren't going to, were you? You were just going to sit here and wallow in your own misery tonight."

I didn't contradict her but figured there was no point in giving her any extra ammunition by confirming her suspicions.

"Did this jerk say all this to his face?" she asked.

I shook my head—as much as I could with her hands still all over it. "He talked over him like he wasn't even there during the meeting but didn't justify himself. Not until after my boss and Fidi had left, at which point he confided all his justifications to me."

Claire relaxed back on her haunches, letting go of my hair and sitting on my knees. "And what did you have to say about that?"

I met her eyes, letting her see all my misery. "Absolutely nothing. My tongue was frozen in my mouth and it was all I could do to get out of there without throwing up on my client's shoes."

She cupped my chin in one hand and let it fall back in her lap. "And now you're feeling guilty."

"Of course I am." I suddenly couldn't sit still anymore. Making sure I didn't hurt her, I dumped Claire back in her seat and sprang up to pace across my small living room. "I just froze, Claire. That jackass was judging Fidi and saying everything was his fault just because he's gay, and I can't even summon a single word to defend him?"

I realized I still had the bottle of beer in my hand and stalked into the kitchen to get an opener. I took a large gulp and went back to pacing across the room while Claire watched me with her compassionate eyes.

"Seriously," I fumed. "We're in the twenty-first century. Why do people like that guy still exist?"

"They've always been around," Claire said calmly, "and most likely always will. We just have to—"

"He's the boss so he gets to decide who's on the project and who isn't? Bullshit! As long as the job gets done, he doesn't have *anything* to say about the how or the who." I threw my hands up in frustration and sent a large spill of beer across the floor. "Bloody hell," I growled as I set my bottle down on the table and grabbed a couple of napkins from a drawer.

"I just can't believe there are still dinosaurs like him around," I complained while I was on all fours on the floor, mopping up my spill. "I've never met such a ridiculous attitude at work, and I've been on my share of projects over the last ten years. To think, I almost—"

Silence as I got the last drops and stalked to the kitchen to get rid of the drenched napkins.

I grabbed my beer and threw myself on the couch again. I could *feel* my face folding into one giant grouchy frown.

"To think you almost what?" Claire asked, her voice calm but careful.

I put a hand to my hair and scratched my fingers back and forth, trying to get the creepy feeling out. "I'm just so *angry*."

"To think you almost what, Tristan?" Claire put a hand on my thigh and bent her head to put herself in my line of vision.

I met her eyes and ground my teeth, feeling like a five-year-old being caught with a hand in the cookie jar. I didn't want to tell her. But I also didn't know *why* I didn't want to tell her.

"Come on, Tristan," she cajoled. "You'll feel better once you tell me."

She was probably right. I needed to talk to *someone* and Claire had always been there for me.

I scratched at the label of my beer, not meeting her eyes. "I thought about coming out to the team," I mumbled.

Claire had been gently caressing my thigh, but now her hand stopped. Her breath caught. "You what?"

I jutted my jaw out, refusing to repeat myself.

"What haven't you told me?" she asked.

"Nothing," I replied, annoyance seeping into my tone. "I just told you everything."

"Uh uh." I could feel her shaking her head. "You told me everything about the work stuff. But there's something personal going on here, too."

"Maybe I just didn't feel like hiding anymore." Yep, sounding nice and defensive.

"Something happened with Fidi, didn't it?"

I wanted to deny it, but the sound coming out of my mouth—something between a sigh and a groan—gave me away. I waited, but Claire was done with her questions. She'd gone over to the very effective method of just waiting for me to talk.

"Fine," I said once I couldn't take the silence anymore. "Something happened with Fidi. But that's not why I was thinking of coming out at work!"

Claire crossed her feet under her to get comfortable in her corner of the couch. "Wasn't it?"

I groaned. "All right. It probably was. But only partly. I mean, it's not like we're even boyfriends or anything."

"Good," Claire said.

"Huh?"

"I'm not saying it's good you're not boyfriends." Claire's voice was full of laughter, but she was laughing with me, not at me. "It's good you want to come out for you, not for somebody else."

I gave her a skeptical look as I took another sip of my beer.

"I'm serious," she said with a friendly punch to my shoulder. "I always thought it was a good idea for you to come out when you felt ready for it, but hinging it on a boyfriend probably wasn't very bright. Especially when your type is the out-and-proud kind."

I chewed on her words. "But what's the point of coming out if I don't even have a boyfriend to show off?" And I had no doubt about having burned all my bridges with Fidi after today.

Claire leaned in to kiss my cheek. "You do it for you, stupid."

I met her eyes. "But what if it ruins my career?"

"It won't. At worst, you find out that your current company is no good and you go looking for a job elsewhere. We live in Toulouse, the fourth biggest city in France, with hundreds of IT companies. I'm fairly certain you'd be able to find a job within a day or two if you sent out a couple of resumes."

She had a point. But I still wasn't convinced I should come out at work. If anything, this whole debacle had proved to me that I wasn't as ready as I'd thought I'd been. I *could* just continue as I always had, keeping my private life private. Perhaps the better solution would be to be open with any future boyfriends about the fact that I wouldn't ever be out at work? At least they'd know what they were getting into.

Soon, Claire had a *Gendarmes* movie lined up, knowing exactly what I needed to take my mind off my woes. We settled down in front of the TV with a simple dish of carbonara and another beer, and soon I was laughing so hard at Louis de Funès that tears were running down my cheeks.

Thank God for good friends.

THIRTY-ONE

Civil and Professional

THE NEXT MORNING, I once again found myself in Dimitri's office.

Fidi was there before me, in the visitor's chair with his laptop on his knees, not meeting my eyes. Dark circles were forming under his eyes—considering his dark skin, I had a feeling that meant he was absolutely exhausted.

I wanted to reach out and smooth the frown from his brows, the circles from under his eyes.

I stayed close to the door, leaning against the wall.

"Fidi," Dimitri said as he crossed his legs and settled into his big office chair. "Give us a quick run-down of yesterday's outing with the police, please."

Fidi nodded. His eyes never left his screen, as if he needed to read the script for what he was about to tell us. "Two officers accompanied me to the meeting at Cédric Massotier's house last night. Once he realized what was going on, he didn't even have anywhere to run. He admitted to filching the data from his cousin's computer some time back and figured he could make a quick buck or two without anyone being the wiser."

The tiniest movement of his head indicated how idiotic he thought the guy was. "He'd copied the database to one USB drive and an external hard drive, so we got both of those." He finally lifted his gaze to meet Dimitri's eyes. "I'm certain there were no other copies. He was totally freaked out by being caught by the police and cooperated fully from the very start."

Dimitri gave a satisfied nod. "Good. At least that's one problem solved." He met my eyes across the room. "Now we just need to calm down the client."

"I'm on it," I said. "I've arranged to buy him lunch today, to give him the good news."

"Excellent." Dimitri's jaw worked as he glanced at Fidi. "Are you both going?"

Fidi finally looked at me. But instead of reassuring me, the flat apathy I saw in his eyes made me try to make a step back—right into the wall.

"I don't think that would be a good idea," Fidi said.

I couldn't get my voice to work. I couldn't bring myself to agree with him—though he was undoubtedly right—because it would mean openly acknowledging the cause of the client's dislike. Had I really thought about coming out just two days ago? I couldn't even bring myself to talk about *Fidi's*, an openly out guy, sexual orientation, and I'd thought I could handle talking about my own?

I really had been kidding myself for years.

Dimitri's fingers tapped a beat on his knee. "His attitude may change for the better once he knows you caught our data thief."

Fidi huffed a mirthless laugh. "I doubt it."

Studying the both of us in turn, Dimitri let the silence settle. I felt like I should say something but didn't know what.

"What haven't you told me?" Dimitri's blue eyes stared at me through his wire-rimmed glasses. "Why will showing Monsieur Houliez that Fidi has caught the culprit not be enough to clear his name?"

Somehow, I found my voice. "Well, I'd never say never, but there's a chance Monsieur Houliez's dislike for Fidi has always been there, he just hid it when everything was running smoothly."

Fidi's eyes were back on his closed laptop, his knuckles going white from grabbing it too hard.

Dimitri's gaze darkened as his gaze slowly ran over Fidi. His gaze flicked back to me as he asked, "Racist?"

I shook my head quickly.

"Hmm." Dimitri rolled his neck. "Can't say I'm not disappointed. Monsieur Houliez has always been an excellent man to work with up until now."

I eased back against the wall as tension I hadn't been aware of eased up a little. I hadn't thought Dimitri had anything against gays, but with the way he'd described Fidi that first day, I just couldn't be sure. To see him angry with the client for discriminating against Fidi allowed me to breathe just a little easier.

Fidi seemed similarly relieved, his hold on his computer easing up. His eyes stayed down, though.

"Maybe I should come along for the lunch meeting," Dimitri said. "Or would you like to handle it on your own, Tristan?"

I gulped. This was probably one of those situations where I was supposed to take charge and show I could handle everything myself, but I felt like I was standing on quicksand. Like, as long as I wasn't open and honest about who I was, I had no right to stand up for Fidi.

I couldn't let my weakness ruin Fidi's career. "I think it would probably be a good idea for you to come," I said. "He didn't have any compunction about talking to me about it the other day, but he kept his mouth shut while you were there. Maybe he realizes that it wasn't right."

"He just didn't want to say it to my face," Fidi said, still in that lifeless voice.

"Would *you* like to come to lunch?" Dimitri asked. "We're both ready to fight for you"—he waved a hand between himself and me—"but if you want to have your say, you're perfectly welcome. So long as it stays civil and professional, of course."

Fidi seemed to really think about it. He looked at Dimitri, out the window, at his hands—and finally at me. His look was impassive as he studied me, making me feel like he saw through me like an X-ray, seeing all the hidden flaws and oddities.

"I think I'll let Tristan fight this battle for me," he said. The unspoken challenge of, *let's see if you're up for it,* clear in the air between us.

"Excellent." Dimitri slapped his hand on the desk and turned his chair to face his computer. "Email me the address of the restaurant, Tristan, and I'll be there."

Nodding, I grabbed blindly for the door handle and after finding it on the third attempt, fled the office.

THIRTY-TWO

The Golden Boy

I PACED OUTSIDE of the restaurant, too nervous to stay still in the shadow of one of the small trees lining the street while I waited for Monsieur Houliez and Dimitri to join me.

Fidi had once again spent the morning working from the tiny meeting room. With most of the leg work for the catastrophe done, it could only mean that he was avoiding me—not that I blamed him.

Dimitri arrived from the parking lot at a brisk pace, his pinstripe suit and purple tie immaculate as always. His glasses glinted in the glaring sun as he approached.

"I gave Fidi some time off next week," he said. "He's done enough overtime over the past month to deserve it, not to mention that meeting."

I nodded mutely. Why hadn't I thought of that?

Because I was too self-centered, in addition to being a coward, that's why.

Dimitri glanced around, making certain the client wasn't there yet. "What exactly did Monsieur Houliez say to you when we'd left the room the other day? How explicit was he?"

I let out an uneven breath. "He didn't use the words gay or homosexual, if that's what you're asking. He just made it very clear that he wouldn't trust guys 'like him,' that they did nothing but party and moisturize and never took anything seriously."

Dimitri's lips pursed in anger. "Not quite explicit, but clear enough. Unfortunately, not enough to be counted as proof if we should attempt to press charges."

My eyebrows shot up. He was thinking of pressing charges? "Wouldn't that be…counterproductive? First, we lose his data, then we press charges when he gets mad?"

"Yes, unfortunately," Dimitri replied. "We do have to think of our reputation and the future of our collaboration with his company." He visibly straightened his shoulders. "But I'll be damned if I let him get away with nothing. That is no way to be treating another human being, be he sub-contractor or colleague, dark-skinned or white, gay or straight."

I couldn't take my eyes off him. I'd always respected Dimitri as a boss—he was fair and efficient and tended to get things done. But I had sold him short on his human side. I'd assumed he'd bow to the client, no matter how mean and unfair he was, putting the company first.

The pressure in my chest eased a little.

Two minutes later, Monsieur Houliez joined us and we entered the restaurant.

It was small and cozy with less than fifteen tables. We were seated in a corner, by a narrow window and just below a wall of wine bottles, mostly reds from the Southwest. Monsieur Houliez took a seat by the window and Dimitri sat next to me opposite him.

A waiter explained the menu and brought us a bottle of water.

"So what's good here?" Monsieur Houliez asked.

"Everything," I replied honestly. "Pick anything from today's specials, and you should be good to go."

This is exactly what all three of us did, and two minutes later we sat sipping a glass of red each while we waited for the starters.

"So," Monsieur Houliez said to Dimitri, "you have good news?"

"Indeed, we do," Dimitri replied. His voice was casual and agreeable, the underlying anger from earlier gone—or at least, well hidden. He nodded for me to do the honors.

"Fidi managed to get the name of the data thief yesterday afternoon," I said. I could have said *we*, as a team, but I really wanted to make it clear that we had results only because Fidi had done a hell of a good job. "He brought the police with him to the guy's house and filed a complaint at the police station when they brought him in.

"The guy confessed even before leaving his house. Fidi is certain he has contained the data leak, and we've identified where he got the data in the first place to make certain that door is securely closed."

Monsieur Houliez considered me over his glass of wine as the liquid sloshed within. "How did he get the data?"

Dimitri answered before I could decide whether I had to out Sylvie or not. "He had access to the laptop of one of our team members. It was a human error, and it won't happen again."

"You're not going to tell me who it was?" Monsieur Houliez's lips thinned to an uneven line across his face.

"No," Dimitri replied, calm as ever.

"It was that Tech Lead of yours, wasn't it? The one with the impossible name." His eyes darted between Dimitri and me, trying to read both of us at once.

I didn't even consider the option of letting that one slide. "It most definitely was not. The data was stolen well before he was even on the project."

Shit. Shouldn't have said that.

Monsieur Houliez lowered his glass to the table and folded his hands on the empty plate in front of him. "How long have you known about the theft?"

Inside, I was shaking, but I managed to keep a cool exterior and an even voice. "We learned about it this week, Monsieur Houliez, just like you. But when we retrieved the data from the thief, we saw the dates for the last save and for the copy." I leaned slightly back in my chair, feigning nonchalance. "It was more than a month before Fidi came on with the team."

Eyes narrowed, it didn't look like Monsieur Houliez believed me, but he also wasn't able to call my bluff.

When I didn't cave under his scrutiny, he turned back to Dimitri. "What are your next steps?"

Dimitri replied as if he didn't hear the anger in his client's voice. "We work closely with the police to aid them in their investigation and to follow up on the case."

"How can I be sure this won't happen again in a month or two? Clearly, the cause was human negligence. There's no reason it won't happen again."

"There most certainly is," I argue. "Though the entire team had received an awareness training on security issues in the past"—small lie, but just on the question of the date—"it's possible they didn't take all the messages to heart. That tends to happen when it's all theoretical. But now that we've had a real incident in the team? None of our team members will be at the source of a data leak again. That I can guarantee."

My speech seemed to mollify Monsieur Houliez somewhat. He took another sip of wine and sat back as the waiter arrived with our starters: gazpacho soup for me, and goat cheese salads for the two others.

"What about application security?" Monsieur Houliez asked around a mouthful of salad.

"It's been in place for a while," I replied. "As promised after the last delivery. Fidi has spent quite some time fine-tuning it"—it galled me to not be able to give him the credit for the whole thing, but that would mean we'd started too late—"and you'll have a detailed report on the number of weaknesses in the code both for the previous delivery and this one. And you'll see the number has gone down drastically." That last bit really should have been sold, not given freely, but it was part of the price we were going to pay to get some of the client's goodwill back.

At the mention of Fidi's name, Monsieur Houliez's mouth twitched down, as if he'd tasted something unpleasant.

Unable to stop myself, I added, "Fidi really has been an exceptional asset to the team, with his vast knowledge of security norms and issues. Did you know he's certified ISO 27001?"

That twitch appeared again.

I took a gulp of wine and met Dimitri's gaze. He'd seen it, too, and he wasn't much happier about it than me.

"I must admit," Dimitri said, voice much calmer than I could have managed, "I was a little surprised by your attitude toward our Tech Lead during our meeting earlier this week. Has there been some issue with him that I've not been informed of?"

Monsieur Houliez's forehead creased into a frown and he kept his eyes on his plate as he chewed. It was impolite to speak with a full mouth, but he seemed to be taking his sweet time.

"Nothing specific," he finally said. A sip of wine. "I'm just not sure he's a good fit for the project."

"What makes you say that?" Dimitri said. I was infinitely grateful he was there, because he was a million times better at acting than me. In fact, if I hadn't seen his reaction earlier, I might have thought he was taking the client's side.

Apparently reassured that we'd listen to reason, Monsieur Houliez took another sip of his wine, taking his time and meeting our gazes this time. "It's a very important project, both for your company and for mine. It needs a certain…maturity. And trust."

Dimitri nodded. "And you do not feel that Fidisoa fills these requirements?"

"I feel he may be too…frivolous…to be a good fit."

"Frivolous?" Dimitri managed to sound only vaguely interested, while I decided to clamp my mouth shut in order to avoid insulting or throttling the client. I focused on my soup.

Monsieur Houliez was starting to feel more at ease for every non-refuted statement. "Surely, you've noticed that he stands out from the rest of the team. I cannot imagine the time he must spend shopping to find men's clothes in so many colors, not to mention the time it must take to fix his hair every morning."

For a straight guy, he'd certainly spent a lot of time observing Fidi.

Don't say a word. Let Dimitri handle it.

Dimitri chewed on his goat cheese as he cocked his head. "I fail to see how this should impact how he does his job for our project. Surely, you agree that nobody's expected to spend *all* their time working. The work day is only seven and a half hours long, give or take a few minutes. If Fidisoa wishes to spend the rest of his time on clothing or his hair, that should be his business."

I could kiss Dimitri for the way he was handling this. So calm and poised—to the point that Monsieur Houliez still hadn't caught on to the fact that Dimitri wasn't ever going to agree with him.

"What about the distraction he is bound to present to the rest of the team?"

"How so?" Dimitri asked. "Because he's wearing bright colors? I'm sure the team can manage the visual distraction."

"What if he…" Monsieur Houliez glanced left and right, as if afraid someone would overhear. "Comes on to other team members?"

My spoon slowed on the way to my mouth. Had anybody told the client about Fidi's ridiculous game of making the straight guys freak out? Was it, finally, going to come back and bite him in the ass—in the most spectacular way possible?

Dimitri showed no reaction, making me think he might not even have heard of Fidi's game. "Well, at least Mesdemoiselles Bernard and Lambert can rest assured that one colleague will not approach them in any inappropriate manner." He tore off a piece of his bread and scooped up the remaining sauce on his plate before shoving it into his mouth. "Not that I think they worry about that much concerning the other men on the team."

"I wasn't talking about the women," Monsieur Houliez said.

"I realize that, Monsieur Houliez," Dimitri replied calmly. "I simply do not agree that Fidisoa is in any way a danger to our project. Quite the contrary. If it weren't for him, there's a good chance our data thief would still not be caught and your data could have ended up in the wrong hands." He fixed Monsieur Houliez with a glare. "He saved all our asses. I will not repay his hard work by kicking him off the team just because you don't like his clothes."

The waiter arrived to take away our empty plates. A tense silence fell over the table while we let him do his job.

I wondered if Monsieur Houliez would realize that Dimitri didn't agree with him and let the matter drop, but it turned out he was even more of a jackass than I'd first thought.

Monsieur Houliez emptied his glass of wine, then spoke as he refilled it. "I do not have a problem with how he dresses. I simply rest convinced that he is not what this team needs."

"Why?" I couldn't stop myself from asking. "What makes him not right?" How would he justify his views without coming out and saying he didn't like Fidi because he was gay? He seemed aware enough to know that he wasn't allowed to discriminate based on sexual orientation. So far, he'd only skirted the line, unfortunately.

Monsieur Houliez took another gulp of wine as he studied me. "Well," he said. "Perhaps I could make my point in a comparison. Let's take how the two of you present yourselves in a meeting with the client." He waved a hand at me to encompass my clothes. "You dress as expected, with classic colors and no extra fuss. Your colleague shows up in a pink shirt and highlights in his hair."

I wondered if I should ask him if he thought Fidi put the highlights in just to mess with him at work, but Monsieur Houliez wasn't done.

"You stay serious during the meeting. Polite. Fitting for the circumstances. *He* keeps smiling and winking, as if our entire project was a joke."

I finally found my voice. "Smiling doesn't mean he takes his work any less seriously, Monsieur Houliez. It just means he has a smiling personality and tends to tag on a smile in pretty much any situation."

Except yesterday, when the client had ignored him during an entire meeting, and I'd failed to stand up for him. It was the first time since I'd met Fidi that he hadn't smiled at least every five minutes. My heart plummeted at the realization.

Monsieur Houliez shook his head. "It's not right. That's not how one behaves in the workplace." He looked around the room, his gaze coming to rest in the far corner. "If you'll excuse me for a minute." He left for the bathroom.

The guilt at how I'd failed Fidi yesterday gnawed at me. It would have been so much easier for me to stand up to the client than for Fidi. First, because I wasn't the one under attack, and second, because I was the Project Manager.

Dimitri sighed into his glass next to me. "I'm not sure we'll get anywhere," he said. "I guess the fact that he sees you as the golden boy could be considered a silver lining."

"If you say so," I said flatly. As if I wanted to spend years working with the man just because he'd taken a shine to me.

My breath caught as an idea hit me. "Actually," I said, "I may have an idea." My heart thundered in my chest and my hand shook as I reached for my glass of water. Could I really do it?

Dimitri glanced behind him and I saw Monsieur Houliez exiting the bathroom. "Go for it," Dimitri said. "If you've got something that can bring him down, I'm one hundred percent behind you."

THIRTY-THREE

My Stupid Plan

THE WAITER CAME back just as Monsieur Houliez took his seat, bringing us our main dishes. I'm usually a big fan of duck, but right now I couldn't fathom the idea of putting anything into my mouth. I was close enough to throwing up as it was.

But I was going through with my stupid plan.

"I'm afraid I still don't quite understand," I said, putting all my energy into not letting my voice quake and give me away. "In what way do you think I'm better a fit for this project than Fidi? After all, we have two quite different jobs, and I couldn't do everything."

"I'm not saying you need to do everything," Monsieur Houliez graciously offered. "And it's not just you. I could make the same point for Olivier or Denis. But you're here, so it's easier to compare. Always give concrete examples," he said as if giving worldly advice.

"Fair enough," I said. "I'm willing to offer myself up as comparison if it will help me understand why you think Fidi isn't right for the project."

Spots of color appeared on Monsieur Houliez's cheeks as he dug into his lasagna. He must be thinking he was well on his way to winning the argument and getting rid of Fidi.

"So we already covered the clothing," Monsieur Houliez begins. "You know how to dress for work, in a way that does not distract others. And the smiling." He was holding up two fingers, as if ticking off points as he talked.

I raised a finger as if I was back in school, though I didn't wait for him to allow me to talk. "To be fair, I do my fair share of smiling at work. I haven't consciously smiled or not smiled in client meetings, though."

He winked at me. "Just the right amount, I assure you."

I suppressed a shudder.

"Then there's how seriously you take your job," Monsieur Houliez continued. "I know you've been working long hours since you started on this project, and it gives results."

"Actually, I think Fidi has stayed longer than me every single day since we started on this project."

He pointed a meaty finger at me. "Just proves you're more efficient."

"He's the one who's implemented the application security stuff, trained all the rest of the team, and caught the thief." I caught myself before I said anything incriminating.

Monsieur Houliez leaned back in his chair as he chewed, a satisfied gleam in his eye. "Because you told him to do it."

"I'm pretty sure he would have done it even if I hadn't told him to." I took a deep breath and mentally shook it off. I was getting a little off track here. "But I guess that's how it can look from the outside." I smiled, letting him interpret that as he wanted.

He took it as me agreeing with him, of course. "You're an excellent element, Tristan." He glanced at Dimitri. "Good call in getting him on the team." Back to me again. "If everyone was like you on this team, I'd be satisfied we were headed in the right direction."

"Mmm." I was scared as hell but decided to take the first step toward the precipice. "Are you certain you don't have a problem with Fidi because he's gay? You do realize that has nothing to do with how he does his job?"

The blush was back but covering his entire neck this time. "I never said anything about him being gay."

"No," I agree. "But it wouldn't be too much of a leap to make that conclusion."

His lips pursed in anger, but he kept his trap shut. He knew he couldn't say it out loud, dammit.

"Fair enough," I said lightly, though I could hardly hear myself talk for the blood rushing in my ears. "Let's assume it has nothing to do with Fidi's sexual orientation. Let me attack this from the other end: you're saying you're happy with me? I've done everything right since I got on the team? No reproach?"

Color fading quickly back to normal, Monsieur Houliez nodded. "That's right. That's what I've been trying to get at. Nothing against your Tech Lead personally. I just prefer your way of handling things."

"Mmm." I closed my eyes briefly before taking the plunge. "Would you still think that if you knew I was gay?"

I heard a tiny intake of breath to my right, but didn't turn to see Dimitri's reaction. I only had eyes for Monsieur Houliez.

He chuckled. "Don't be ridiculous."

I said nothing, just sat there studying him. My duck was growing colder by the second, but I'd just have to get by on a bowl of soup for today. My stomach wasn't going to accept any more food right now.

As the seconds went past, I enjoyed watching his mounting nervousness. He tried drinking from an empty glass of wine, then his left eye went off on a series of ticks, making it look like he was winking at me. Wouldn't he find that embarrassing?

"You should watch what you're saying," he finally said. "You never know who's listening."

"What would I care who's listening?" I said with a shrug. "I'm not ashamed of who I am." I was oddly relieved to discover that this was indeed true, even at work. My heart was still beating a thousand beats a minute, though.

Monsieur Houliez pointed his finger at me again. "You're not gay."

So this was what denial looked like in its purest form. It wasn't pretty.

"I got my first girlfriend when I was twelve," I said.

Monsieur Houliez nodded in satisfaction, happy I was proving him right.

"Didn't work out," I said with a shrug. "She just didn't do it for me. Jeff, who sat right behind me in class, though? He definitely did."

Monsieur Houliez's face fell in shock. Ah, was I finally getting through to him?

"I've had"—I pretend to count on my fingers—"maybe eight or nine boyfriends since then. Once I got a taste of boy, I never looked back." Okay, now I was just taunting him.

And it was working. He was white as a sheet, his mouth hung open, and I could see his pulse speeding along on his throat. Probably worrying about all the compliments he'd given me.

"Don't worry," I tell him in all seriousness. "You're not my type."

Last straw. Monsieur Houliez slapped his napkin on the table and shoved back his chair. He turned to Dimitri. "This is not the type of behavior I expected from you and your team," he said in clipped tones.

"I could tell you the same thing," Dimitri replied calmly. "If you have grievances against my people, feel free to tell me about them. But they must be more convincing that what I've seen here today—and they better not be because of anybody's sexual preferences."

Monsieur Houliez stormed out of the restaurant, and I slumped down in my chair, my head in my hands.

What had I just done?

THIRTY-FOUR

This Was How It Was Supposed to Go

"You should eat," Dimitri said after an excruciating minute of silence.

I had bile coming up my throat just at the thought.

I could still backtrack. It was possible to tell Dimitri I'd told the client I was gay only to prove a point. To stand by Fidi.

Just last night I'd concluded that I'd never come out to my colleagues, after years of telling myself that I'd do it when I met the right guy. And here I was, outing myself to a homophobic client just to prove a point.

"I have to admit," Dimitri said as he calmly ate his duck. "I didn't see where you were going until the very end there."

I should tell him it wasn't true.

"It's true," I blurted. Apparently my subconscious wasn't about to let me slip back into the closet.

Dimitri chuckled in response. Once he finished chewing, he continued as if I hadn't spoken. "Not sure I'd have advised you to go that route if we'd discussed it beforehand, but I think you actually got your point across to him."

I lifted my head from my hands to meet his eyes.

He gave me a lopsided smile, then went back to his usual non-smiling self. There was no disgust in his eyes, no judgment in the way he talked to me. *This* was how it was supposed to go when you came out. Meaning nothing changes.

"I'll probably need to go quite soon to do some damage control," Dimitri said. "But I'm not about to let him ruin my meal."

I gulped. "What do you think will happen now?"

"I have no idea what he'll do." Dimitri pointed his fork in direction of the door where Monsieur Houliez had stormed out. "But I'll make sure the management on our side is aware of the discriminatory source of our conflict with the client, so there's no doubt for anyone on whose side they should be on."

Some of the tension in my chest eased at his words and my throat relaxed enough to accept some wine.

"I'll also contact Monsieur Houliez's boss," Dimitri continued, his voice harder. "I'm guessing we'll be avoiding talking directly of the topic at hand in order to avoid any lawsuits, but you will either have an apology or a new client by the end of the week." He met my eyes over the tops of his glasses. "I promise."

Gulping, I nodded. "Thank you."

Dimitri pointed at my untouched food. "Now eat."

Deciding I wasn't going to let an asshat like Monsieur Houliez deprive me of food, I dug in.

THIRTY-FIVE

Kill Me Now

When I got back to the office, Fidi still wasn't in his seat.

"Has he moved permanently to that meeting room?" I asked Sylvie.

She glanced at the empty chair and lifted a shoulder. "He comes in whenever anyone has a question, but yeah, he seems to have set up camp down the hall."

I sighed. "Can you get everyone to meet in here in two minutes, please? I'll go get Fidi."

"How'd the meeting with the client go?" she yelled after me as I left the room.

"That's what I'm gathering everyone for," I yelled back.

Fidi was bent over his laptop, typing away at top speed when I entered. His brows shot down into a V when he saw me. "Now what?"

I longed for the days when Fidi had been playful and flirty twenty-four hours a day. Unfortunately, the stupid client was only partially to blame.

Perhaps I could undo some of the damage.

"Meeting with the whole team in our office in two minutes," I told him. "Be there."

"Sure thing, *chef!*" he yelled after me. Nothing playful about the way he called me boss this time.

Two minutes later, the entire team gathered, looking at me expectantly. Fidi chose a spot as far away from me as possible.

Dimitri had told me I didn't need to inform the team of everything that had gone down with the client over lunch, but I didn't want to give myself an out. If I went home tonight without telling them, I'd never do it. And all of a sudden, I really wanted to. Couldn't take another day of hiding.

"So how'd the meeting go?" Sylvie repeated once everyone was calm.

"Awful," I replied honestly.

Except for possibly Fidi, nobody had expected that answer. I heard a few gasps and suddenly had everybody's undivided attention.

"It actually started yesterday," I explain. "When Monsieur Houliez decided everything bad to have ever happened on this project was Fidi's fault."

Across the room, Fidi stood leaning against the window frame, arms crossed and eyes on his feet.

"He wasn't very clear on the reason for his dislike during the meeting," I said. "But once Dimitri and Fidi were out of the room, he lost no time in explaining to me that someone *like him* had nothing to do on such a high-profile project."

If it weren't for the computers whirring and the air conditioning humming above us, you could have heard the proverbial pin drop.

"Does that mean what I think it does?" Olivier leaned forward in his chair, as if ready to run out to wring the bad guy's neck once I gave him the go.

I glanced around the room, meeting everybody's eyes. "It does," I replied. "Of course, he's aware he's not allowed to discriminate like that, so he never actually worded it in an explicit manner."

"That bastard." Olivier's hands squeezed the armrests of his chair so tight, I feared the furniture might not make it.

"Yes," I agreed. "Then Fidi found our data thief and I had a meeting with Monsieur Houliez a couple of hours ago, to give him the good news. And to attempt to clear Fidi's name. Not that I had much hope of that working." I took a deep breath. "I wasn't too confident about standing up to the client alone, so Dimitri accompanied me."

I managed a small smile. "Just so you know, Dimitri is completely on our side on this issue, and was just as outraged as you are by Monsieur Houliez's position."

Fidi glanced up at that and I thought I read some relief in his eyes before he lowered them again.

I plowed on, even though I couldn't really feel my fingers anymore. Even the day I'd come out to my dad, I hadn't been this nervous. "Needless to say, the client was no happier with Fidi today, even though I explained that he was the one who'd saved us from an even bigger scandal."

I no longer registered the movements around me. I didn't really need them, I just needed to get the words out.

"So I set him up," I said. "I had him compare me and Fidi, getting him to say that I'd have been better than him for everything, despite me having a much less technical background than him."

I took one last deep breath and fixed my gaze on a spot on the wall above Sylvie. "Then I told him I'm gay, too."

A large bang sounded from one corner of the room, and though I really didn't want to meet anyone's eyes, I looked.

Fidi lay flat on the floor, his feet having apparently slipped and dumped him unceremoniously in a heap. He leaped back up and resumed his place, arms crossed and eyes on the floor.

"Monsieur Houliez had much the same reaction," I joked. "Though he flew out the door rather than to the floor."

When no comments were forthcoming, I forced myself to look around the room.

Laure was adjusting her barrette but gave me a huge smile. Denis, right next to her had a similar, though more tamped-down, expression.

Olivier's mouth hung open and his body had gone completely still. "For real?" he said. "Or did you do that just to prove a point?"

Sylvie's hand came out of nowhere and smacked him over the head. "Of course it's real, idiot. How blind can you get?"

At my quizzical look, Sylvie raised an eyebrow. "Did you really think you were hiding it? That's so cute."

Normally, I'd have reacted to being called cute, but right now I was too numb.

The hit to the head had brought Olivier back to the living, but he still wasn't quite following. "So, do you have, like, a… boyfriend, or something?"

Somehow, getting the same old questions brought some of my wits back. "Really? You think I'd have flirted like that with Fidi if I had a boyfriend?"

Everybody's gazes snapped to Fidi, who stood stock still with a deer-in-the-headlights expression, apparently hoping that if he didn't move, we wouldn't see him.

"But that was just a game…" Mathieu seemed to be having as much trouble as Olivier. It was always the guys who thought you were one of them. They just couldn't wrap their minds around it.

"That was kind of the point," I said as I scuffed my foot into the floor. "Hiding in plain sight, so to speak."

"Sorry, honey," Sylvie said, "but you really weren't hiding all that well."

I just shrugged.

"You two shared a room at that cabin." A smirk settled on Olivier's face. Apparently, he just needed some time to adjust, but wasn't going to freak out. "That must have been a lot more interesting than we first thought."

I could feel my face flame as I kept my mouth shut.

"That was not why I told you this," I said, my voice tense.

"Yeah, yeah," Olivier said as he waved my comment away. "Client's a jackass and Dimitri's taking care of it. I'm much more interested in what's going on between you two." He pointed to Fidi, then to me. His shit-eating grin was mirrored on almost everyone in the room.

"Nothing's going on," I said firmly. "And it's none of your business."

Olivier's entire body shook as he laughed. "You've been blatantly flirting in front of the team for weeks, and now you tell us to shove it?" He shook his head. "I think not."

"What do you want me to say?" I flailed my arms as my face blazed and my heart tried to climb out of my throat. "He's awesome, but I blew it because I'm a coward? How would you like it if—"

I didn't see Fidi move until he was in my face. "Better late than never," he said. And crushed his lips to mine.

All thoughts of the rest of the team flew, as my brain latched on to one single thought. *He forgave me?* And I didn't even have to think to pull my arms around him and return the kiss, it was second nature.

I crashed backward, hitting my back in the cupboard before slamming into the wall.

I heard whoops and catcalls but was too busy kissing Fidi to care. I wasn't quite sure this was real and wanted to touch him while I could.

Silence. Someone clearing his throat.

My brain came back online for long enough to realize I should perhaps have a look around.

Dimitri stood in the open door, an eyebrow cocked and his lips twitching as he fought a smile.

I detached my lips from Fidi's and righted us so we stood side by side, gasping. I let one arm stay at his waist, though. I wasn't about to let him think I was embarrassed.

"No need to stop on my account," Dimitri said. "I just stopped by to see what the noise was all about. Keep up the good work." And he left the room.

Kill me. Kill me now.

Laughter broke out, Olivier slapping his thigh in mirth and Sylvie drying off tears as she bent in half.

"Team morale is looking up," Fidi said. Even with his dark skin, I could tell he was blushing at least as much as I was, but he also looked happy. Carefree, like before the awful business with Monsieur Houliez.

I pulled on his hand to get him to meet my eyes. "Hey," I almost whispered so nobody else would overhear. "So I'm no longer in the closet at work."

His eyes glinted at me. "I noticed."

"How are my chances of getting a date with you this week?" My tone was light, but I was sure he could read the nervousness in my stance.

He chewed on his lip as he studied me. "Looking up," he said with a shy smile. "I'll have to check my schedule."

I leaned in to steal another kiss, but as the hooting and catcalls started again, I quickly pulled away. Kissing at work wasn't exactly encouraged, anyway.

"I'm free whenever," I whispered in Fidi's ear. Then I faced the room, red cheeks notwithstanding. "All right, people. Show's over. Now get back to work."

I don't think anybody did anything productive that afternoon. Least of all me.

THIRTY-SIX

I'm Okay with Kissing in the Car

Fidi was waiting for me by my car when I left for the day.

"Any chance of getting a ride?" he asked. He'd placed his bag on the roof of my car and stood leaning against the hood, highlights catching the setting sun.

I didn't even try to fight the smile that took over my face. "Where to?"

He rolled his shoulders. "Wherever." He chewed on his lower lip, making me lose track of the conversation. I could have stood there looking at him all night and never complained.

"Your place?" he said.

My grin got even wider. "Whatever you want, Fidi. I don't mind driving you home to Albi."

He pushed away from the car and stepped toward me. "I'd kind of like to see your place."

I swallowed as Fidi stopped right in front of me. If I leaned in, I could kiss him. "My place it is," I whispered.

I glanced around us, at the other cars in the parking lot and the hundreds of office windows surrounding us. My body warred between leaning in for a kiss and taking a step back.

"I'm not backtracking or anything," I said as I stared beseechingly into his gorgeous eyes. "But I'm not really comfortable with making out in the company parking lot."

Fidi's eyes flickered to the building behind me. His smile never wavered. "Yeah, I kind of agree. Making out in front of the entire team is also not something I usually do."

I chuckled. "Good. I'm guessing we're going to need some ground rules." I unlocked the car and Fidi walked around to the passenger side to get in.

"I'm okay with kissing in the car," I said once we'd both closed our doors.

"Me, too." Fidi leaned over and brushed his lips over mine. The kiss was soft, feather light, and carried the promise of many more to come.

I traced a finger along his jaw and across his full lips. I couldn't believe I was allowed to do that, and without any pretenses. "I'm sorry I didn't stand up for you yesterday," I said.

He grabbed my hand and squeezed it. "Don't worry about it. I should have stood up for myself." He shook his head and leaned back against the headrest. "I claim to fight for gay rights and when I'm actually face to face with that kind of hate, I just turn tail and run?"

I turned the ignition and started easing out of my parking spot. "It wasn't exactly clear why he didn't like you during that meeting."

Fidi huffed. "If it wasn't the gay thing it would have been the skin color thing. In any case, it's not cool."

"True." I waved to Sylvie, who was about to enter her own car. She winked at me when she saw my passenger. "But it's not always easy to fight back straight away when you're taken by surprise like that."

Fidi tilted his head so he was looking at me instead of at the road. "You did good, though."

I shook my head. The praise just didn't sit right with me. "Dimitri's doing the real work. I just blurted out that I'm gay."

Fidi laughed, as if I'd done something precious. "For you, that's huge."

I blew out a breath. "Sad, but true."

"I'm proud of you." Fidi placed his hand on mine on the gearstick and gave it a squeeze. He shifted in his seat. "I went to talk to Dimitri this afternoon."

"Yeah?" I glanced at him, trying to gauge his mood.

"Asked him to put me on a new project."

"What?" The giddy feeling from a second ago dissipated as I worried this *would* affect his career after all. "Why?"

"Calm down," Fidi said, laughter in his voice. "Don't drive us off the road. The team doesn't really need me anymore. Everything is in place and Denis is more than capable of maintaining it. I didn't like how I basically stole his job."

"But—"

"And more importantly," he continued, "I'm not a big fan of office romances."

"Oh." I felt my face heat at his implications, both past and future. "But…will you be going back to Albi?" A one-hour drive wasn't exactly insurmountable, but right now it felt too far.

He gave my hand another squeeze. "I asked him to find me another project here in Toulouse. Guess I'll have to start looking for a new place to live."

I stole a look at him out of the corner of my eye.

"Don't worry!" He barked a laughter. "That is *not* me trying to hedge my way into living with you." He chuckled some more, apparently finding the idea hilarious. "I wouldn't mind some help in hunting for a place, though."

My heart swelled with affection—and probably another, stronger feeling that I hadn't felt in a really long time. "I know this really nice part of town where you should totally try to find an apartment."

"Are we on our way there, by any chance?"

"Yes, we are."

Fidi pulled my hand into his lap and covered it with both of his. "Sounds perfect."

Author's Note

THANK YOU FOR reading Fidi and Tristan's story! If you enjoyed the book, I hope you'll consider leaving an honest review somewhere, to help other readers find the book.

This story was first published in 2019 under a pen name. It seemed like a good idea at the time, but I've discovered I do not have the patience or will to have two social media presences, so I've decided to bring all my books under one name.

If you want to stay updated on any new stories, I invite you to sign up for my newsletter on rwwallace.com. You can opt in or out of the genres you're interested in, so you can get updates only on romance books for example, or add in mystery...you can even choose to get information (in French) about French translations!

The next book in the *French Office Romance* series is Laure and Denis' story. It's called Hiding in Plain Sight and will be available at all the major retailers not long after this one.

R.W. Wallace
rwwallace.com

Also by R.W. Wallace

Romance

French Office Romance Series
Flirting in Plain Sight
Hiding in Plain Sight
Loving in Plain Sight
(tie-in short story, available through newsletter)

Mystery

Ghost Detective Novels
Beyond the Grave

Ghost Detective Shorts
Just Desserts
Lost Friends
Family Bonds
Common Ground
Till Death
Family History
Heritage
Eternal Bond
New Beginnings

The Tolosa Mystery Series
The Red Brick Haze
The Red Brick Cellars
The Red Brick Basilica

Short Stories
Cold Blue Eternity

Hidden Horrors
Critters
Gertrude and the Trojan Horse
First Impressions
Let Them Eat Cake
Out of Sight
Sitting Duck
Two's Company
Like Mother Like Daughter

Fantasy (short stories)
Unexpected Consequences
Morbier Impossible
A Second Chance

Science Fiction (short stories)
The Vanguard

Lollapalooza Shorts
Quarantine
Common Enemies
Coiled Danger
Mars Meeting

Adventure (short stories)
Size Matters

About the Author

R.W. Wallace writes in most genres, though she tends to end up in mystery more often than not. Dead bodies keep popping up all over the place whenever she sits down in front of her keyboard. Except when a romance just *has* to come out. Or when a whole new fantasy world is taking form in her mind... You get the point.

The stories mostly take place in Norway or France; the country she was born in and the one that has been her home for two decades. Don't ask her why she writes in English—she won't have a sensible answer for you.

Her Ghost Detective short story series appears in *Pulphouse Magazine*, starting in issue #9.

You can find all her books, long and short, all genres, on her website: rwwallace.com.

www.ingramcontent.com/pod-product-compliance
Lightning Source LLC
LaVergne TN
LVHW041705060526
838201LV00043B/578